49601

D0331253

THE
SHADOW MAN

THE
SHADOW MAN

by
John Lutz

WILLIAM MORROW AND COMPANY, INC.
New York   *1981*

Library of Congress Cataloging in Publication Data

Lutz, John, 1939–
    The shadow man.

    I. Title.
PS3562.U854S48   813'.54   80-27157
ISBN 0-688-00459-8   AACR1

Printed in the United States of America

First Edition

1   2   3   4   5   6   7   8   9   10

For Steve, Jennifer and Wendy . . .
In that disorder

THE
SHADOW MAN

1

Senator Jerry Andrews had voted against the water appropriations bill. He supported the concept of the bill, but there were some amendments that the President damn well knew would prove costly to the already impoverished over the next several years. So the much needed bill was stalled, possibly for months. Sometimes politics was pure crap.

After adjournment, Andrews left the Senate Chamber immediately. Now he walked along the well-lighted corridor toward his offices in the Senate Office Building. He was a tall, energetic man suspended between the loose-jointed affability of youth and the graying distinction of middle age. His athletic body seemed tailored for his conservative three-piece suit, rather than the other way around, and his straight brown hair was just beginning to be shot with silver. But he still had a persistent cowlick near the crown of his head, and at times his lanky frame seemed to contain too much youthful vitality for the traditional sedateness of his surroundings. During the past two years he had been involved in several bitterly fought political frays, and the strain had left its imprint on his lean, habitually amiable features—deeper lines from his nose to the corners of his ever more resolute lips, faint crow's-feet radiating from the corners of his candid gray eyes. Lately those eyes had taken on a somber, level gaze that caught even Andrews by surprise some mornings as he stood shaving before his mirror. He was indeed beginning to look like a United States senator. And in the past few years he finally had come to feel like one.

Several people nodded to him as they passed in the long corridor. Andrews was becoming well known in Washington. He was not yet a national figure, but he now knew that soon he would be. The senior members of the Senate, the news media, were watching him, had tagged him as an increasingly important factor in the equation and were still trying to bracket him for reference. In this city, everything and everyone had to be labeled.

"Senator!" Wayne Hallock of Iowa called, smiling as he approached. "How are you going to explain that water appropriations vote at home?"

Andrews returned the elderly senator's wily grin. "I don't think I'll have to, as long as my wife has enough to wash and cook."

Hallock snorted and brushed a strand of wispy white hair back from his eyes. "I mean, how are you going to explain it to your constituents? Or haven't you seen the latest polls from your great state?"

"Explaining is my business," Andrews said easily. He squeezed Hallock's bony arm in friendly parting and continued down the corridor, his footsteps echoing rhythmically as he approached his office. He had the feeling that Hallock was still watching him, calculating how to convince him to accept the President's amendments on the stalled bill. And on the mental balance sheet that every politician kept, Andrews owed Hallock.

As Andrews neared his office door, his appointments secretary, Judy Carnegie, rounded a corner and strode toward him hugging a bulging legal-size portfolio to her breast with both arms, as if she were carrying an infant. Judy always walked with swift deliberation, giving the impression that she was almost but not quite late for an appointment. And her dark eyes always glittered with eagerly mischievous intelligence beneath her bangs, reflecting the pragmatic machinations that regularly went on behind them. Just five years out of Vassar, she had come far. She had aspirations.

"Busy, busy," she chanted with a grin, somehow balancing her burden and opening the office door for Andrews. "Hey, wait'll you hear your schedule for the rest of the day. A killer."

"Beats having lost the election," Andrews told her, rankling her by stepping aside so she would have to enter first. Men didn't make even the slightest allowances for femininity in Judy's yearned-for world.

Andrews' office was medium-sized, sparsely but expensively furnished, cluttered with the accoutrements of his profession. On one wall were framed various awards that Andrews had received throughout his career. On another hung a large autographed portrait of the President, wearing his firm but friendly expression. The walls were light green and freshly painted.

Judy dropped the heavy portfolio onto a small library table while Andrews stripped off his suit coat and loosened his tie. "What is all that junk?" he asked, pointing to the portfolio.

"The transcripts of every speech Walter Gorham has made since nineteen forty-five," she said. "And miscellaneous information pertaining to the economy."

Andrews looked closely at Judy and nodded slowly and admiringly. Walter Gorham was soon to come before the Senate for confirmation as Federal Reserve Board chairman. By that time, Andrews would have studied the information Judy had compiled and know not only how to vote, but how to cope with the potential assets and liabilities that went along with that vote, be it aye or nay.

He sat behind his desk and leaned back in his upholstered swivel chair as Judy opened the large, leather-bound appointment book and studied it. "Lunch at one with Senator Davis," she said, "then at three you meet with Frank Turner in his office to discuss the campaign fund bill. At four you have an appointment here with a representative of the American Save the Wicker Society—"

"The *what?*" Andrews interrupted.

Judy shrugged. "Four thirty is the long-distance call from Masters in California. Five thirty you meet Governor Vincent for cocktails at Ricardo's."

Andrews sighed. The only possible free time in the schedule was after lunch with Davis, but Davis was notorious for his prolonged, alcoholic lunches.

"And your wife phoned and wants to speak with you," Judy added in an automatically neutral tone.

They both knew that Ellen was Andrews' principal political liability. But Ellen also realized that and played the game. Or had so far.

Andrews rose from behind his desk and walked into the small washroom to splash cool water on his face and brace himself for the rest of the day. Hadn't he asked for this in hundreds of campaign speeches?

"Dial Ellen for me," he instructed Judy, shoving the washroom door closed with his foot.

"One other thing," Judy called from the office. "Dr. Dana Larsen phoned. He asked to see you as soon as it was convenient."

"About?"

"Didn't say."

Andrews paused, letting his hands remain beneath the stream of cold water. "Did you work him in?"

"For ten tomorrow morning. He's flying into town on an early flight."

When Andrews had freshened up for his lunch with Davis and returned to his desk, Judy informed him that Ellen hadn't answered her phone. Relieved, he told her not to bother calling again.

Then he put down the papers he was to sign and wondered why Dr. Dana Larsen wanted an appointment. Three months ago Andrews had used his influence for Larsen, who was a psychiatrist and an old college friend, to obtain entree to interview convicted political assassin Martin Karpp in a maximum-security asylum for the criminally insane in New York. Larsen was doing research on the phenomenon of multiple personality, and Karpp had come to be regarded as a classic case, a man who possessed six distinctly separate personalities. Other than having read a few popularized histories of such cases, Andrews knew nothing about the subject. The favor was one of the few Larsen had ever asked of Andrews; he considered the series of interviews with Karpp essential to his work.

An instinctive caution alarm was silently signaling in the back of Andrews' mind. Larsen might possibly stir up some bizarre new angle on the Governor Drake assassination. Though the murder had been carefully investigated and tirelessly discussed, and though there was absolutely no doubt as to Karpp's guilt, always there were the conspiracy fanatics. Even the John Kennedy assassination, now rightfully the property of history, was still being picked over by those intrepid nonbelievers.

Of course Dana Larsen was one of the most reasonable and professionally responsible men Andrews knew. That was why Andrews had decided to pull strings and get him the interviews with Karpp. But now Andrews found himself questioning that decision. The Drake assassination still was a delicate subject, especially in the South.

One of the lucite buttons on Andrews' desk phone began to blink, then dimmed as Judy answered at her desk.

"Your wife again, Senator," she told Andrews.

He drew a deep breath, as if seeking precious oxygen, and lifted the receiver. Maintaining a political career was like juggling vials of nitroglycerin.

2

In a small hexagonal gray room at the Belmont Institution for the Criminally Insane, Dr. Dana Larsen sat facing Martin Karpp. Between them was a narrow oak table covered with nicks and time-darkened scars, almost luminous with a patina created by years of the perspiration and despair of intent conversation.

Over the black frames of his glasses, Larsen calmly observed Karpp. The political assassin seemed composed, his square-shouldered, stocky frame relaxed as he drummed idly, yet with a curious sort of detached concentration, on the table with sturdy, blunt fingers.

The man fascinated Larsen, as did the general subject of multiple personality. So little was known about the affliction, and so much might be garnered from more understanding of its genesis. And Martin Karpp embodied a rare opportunity for serious study.

"Tell me more about Jay Jefferson," Dr. Larsen suggested.

Karpp's black eyebrows rose as he considered this request. His face was heavy-featured but symmetrical, not unhandsome in a thick, brooding fashion. He seemed to enjoy discussing his various personalities, talking about them as if they were acquaintances, sometimes old friends. And always he referred to them in the third person. Larsen had never spoken to

Martin Karpp when Karpp was anyone but his genuine identity. But it was "Jay Jefferson" who four years ago had shot presidential candidate Governor Hugh Drake, and who inadvertently had been betrayed at the trial by Martin Karpp. That Karpp and Jay Jefferson occupied the same body, along with four other identities, had resulted in an insanity decree and Karpp's confinement for life here at Belmont.

"Jay had to shoot the governor," Karpp said, after slow consideration. "He's sorry he had to kill. But he's also sorry that people don't understand he did it for his country, for the way of life that everyone but a few people like Jay, with the guts to see things as they really are, takes for granted."

"But what gave him the idea of assassinating the governor?" Larsen asked, leaning forward with unfeigned interest.

Karpp's dark eyes slid off to the side as he smiled. "Are you trying to get me to say something incriminating, Doctor? Underestimating me?"

"You must understand that isn't so," Larsen said. He knew that Karpp had an IQ well above the median. "You're here for the rest of your life anyway. What difference does it make what you say?"

Karpp continued to smile but didn't speak.

Beyond him, on the other side of a clear Plexiglas partition, stood a guard in civilian clothing. The guard was well out of earshot. Karpp knew that. He'd insisted upon it when laying down the conditions for the sessions with Larsen. It had interested Larsen, the way Karpp was able to use what little bargaining position he had and imposed his will.

"He dresses like you," Karpp said, motioning with his head toward the stoic figure of the guard, "but he carries a gun beneath his suit coat."

Larsen nodded. "This is a maximum-security institution. You're considered a dangerous man."

"Not me. Jay."

"How do you feel about that?" Larsen asked. "About Jay

shooting Governor Drake and you being confined for the crime."

Karpp's blocky shoulders moved slightly in a resigned shrug. "I understand how it is."

"You mean about occupying the same body?"

Karpp nodded.

"You've understood since you were eighteen, haven't you?" Larsen said, referring to the findings of the battery of government psychiatrists who had examined Karpp four years ago. They had put him through every test conceivable to substantiate his psychosis. And there was no doubt as to the validity of his fragmented psyche. By the date of the trial's suspension, each of Karpp's five other personalities had even been identified by name.

"I was about eighteen when sometimes I became Alan Hobson," Karpp said. "Alan liked to steal. I was strictly against it, you understand, and tried to talk him out of it. But he said he wanted things—no, he *needed* things. Since he felt so strongly about it, and saw other people stealing in so many ways, he decided it was all right to go ahead. I always pretended he'd bought things when he brought them home and I'd find them in the morning."

"So you don't approve of stealing."

"Of course not."

"How can you approve of murder?"

"I thought I explained about Jay. What if somebody had killed Hitler before he gained power? What about that?"

"How do you feel about Willy Bennet?" Larsen asked, ignoring Karpp's question.

"I feel that what he does is his business. Willy can't help it he's a queer."

"But you don't approve."

"Of homosexuality? I don't know. Like I said, it doesn't concern me. It's Willy's business."

"Does Jay Jefferson approve of Willy's sexual preference?"

Karpp knitted his dark eyebrows. "I don't know. What does it matter?"

Again Larsen ignored Karpp's question. It would be easy to fall into the role of subject rather than interviewer. He wondered if the tragic man across the table was consciously trying to wrest control of the interview from him. Larsen carefully broached the matter he'd been trying to bring into focus for almost a week.

"What about Paul Liggett's note?"

Karpp seemed almost to smile. Paul Liggett was another of his personalities. And a week ago someone had left a note at the desk of Larsen's motel, suggesting rather ominously that he leave the area. The note had been signed Paul Liggett.

"So Paul left you a message," Karpp said matter-of-factly. "So what? Why do we keep getting back to that?"

"If Jay Jefferson can't leave the asylum, how can Paul Liggett?"

Now Karpp did smile, but very faintly. "Maybe Jay can leave. You're the one who said he couldn't. Maybe it isn't right that he's here for what he did, and he *can* leave. Maybe Paul can leave too. Maybe he does. I don't always remember what everyone does; most of the time I don't. Paul shouldn't be here to begin with. Don't you agree?"

"Who did Jay Jefferson know in New York?" Larsen asked.

"The people the FBI found out about. Some I know from what Jay told me in notes. Political people. He'd naturally have friends like that. What else would you expect?"

Karpp had raised his voice slightly in exasperation. Behind him, the plainclothes guard stirred and stood away from the anteroom's tiled wall.

"Why should the question upset you, Martin?" Larsen asked Karpp. "I only want to know so I can talk with these people, find out some things for my research. I told you that, and you agreed to help. I've been honest with you." Larsen emphasized the word honest.

Karpp clamped his lips together and held his large head in his hands as if it were dangerously fragile. He sat that way for a long time. From outside came the faint sound of jays chattering on the grounds. Sunlight, packed with a swirling riot of dust, silently lanced through a narrow, high window and spotlighted the top of the wall to Karpp's left. So intense was the ray of sun that it seemed a man could leap up, grasp it and hang supported by its warm strength and solidity.

"I'm tired, is all," Karpp mumbled at last.

"I'll leave now, then," Larsen said agreeably, switching off the cassette recorder on the corner of the table. "There's no big rush about what we have to say to each other."

Karpp laughed his low, oddly melodic chuckle. "*I* have plenty of time, anyway," he said. "Are you coming back tomorrow?"

"Not tomorrow," Larsen said. "I have another appointment. But I'll be back in a few days." Larsen glanced at Karpp. The stern-featured man appeared to be in his midthirties, though he was now only twenty-seven. Larsen sensed an unspoken regret in Karpp that their usual conversation wouldn't take place tomorrow. He felt an unprofessional pang of pity for this trapped and unfathomable man. Sad bender of history. "Maybe Wednesday," Larsen said, packing recorder and papers into his briefcase.

Smiling at Karpp, Larsen said goodbye and opened the door to step into the guard area.

"You're my only visitor, you know," Karpp said behind him.

Larsen looked at him and nodded. "I'll return, Martin."

"I'm not so sure."

Larsen closed the door and the guard opened the thick outer door for him and stood to one side. The bulge beneath the man's armpit was noticeable and remotely threatening. Before stepping through to the main corridor, Larsen turned and spoke to the guard.

"This might sound naïve," he said, watching the guard's placid, tanned face, "but is there any way he could get out of here?"

The face remained expressionless, making the voice all the more incredulous. "You mean out of the asylum?"

Larsen nodded, shifted his leather briefcase to his left hand.

"There's someone watching him every minute of the day," the guard assured Larsen.

"And night?"

"He's looked in on." A glimmer of light transfixed the guard's eyes, as if he'd suddenly spotted something in Larsen that inspired confidence. "If you're worried about the possibility of escape, forget it. This is maximum security. It might not look it, for the sake of some of the patients and their families, but this place is guarded better than Leavenworth." He said again slowly, as if in irrefutable finality, "Maximum security."

Larsen thanked the guard and glanced through the clear Plexiglas into the interview room. Karpp already had been removed.

As he drove from the grounds of the secluded asylum, Larsen noted again the unobtrusive but numerous safeguards. The high, wire-meshed, barred windows recessed in ivy-covered brick walls, the many white-coated attendants Larsen knew were armed and well trained, the surrounding high double fences with their guarded gates. And outside the sanitarium were miles of heavily wooded hill country, beautiful country violated only by the two-lane blacktop road snaking to the asylum from the nearest town, Carltonville. Even keeping to the road, it would take someone on foot hours to reach the town, hours during which the escape attempt would be discovered and the area sealed and searched. The logical mind balked at the idea that escape from the Belmont sanitarium was possible. The logical mind.

The last of the high gates swung open for Larsen, and he

pressed his foot down on the accelerator of his rented Chevy, then made a hard left turn onto the blacktop road. The tires squealed in a brief, almost human cry of agony.

In his cabin at the Clover Motel, where he was staying just outside of Carltonville, Larsen listened to the tape of his latest conversation with Karpp. Then he spent some time at the small oak writing desk, organizing his notes.

At seven o'clock he left his cabin and drove half a mile down the highway to the Chicken Barn, where he usually had dinner. The small family-owned and -operated restaurant served a variety of good food besides their specialty of crispy fried chicken.

"The veal tonight," he told Carla, the waitress, when she approached his table near the window. "And iced tea."

"Hot as the Lord makes 'em out there today," Carla said, commenting as she invariably did on the weather. The temperature outside was still in the eighties, and Larsen wondered if Carla would have remarked on a cold snap if he'd ordered coffee.

She tucked pad and pencil into the oversized front pocket of her frilly yellow apron, and her long face broke into its horsey yet strangely attractive smile. Her lank, shoulder-length hair added to the impression of total elongation. As she started to leave to deliver the order to the kitchen, she turned.

Now, Larsen was sure, she would ask whether he wanted baked potato or fries.

"Fella was in here earlier lookin' for you," she said, surprising him.

Larsen's hand left the sugar dispenser he'd been toying with. "What fellow?"

"Didn't leave a name. But he knew your name."

"What did he say?"

"Just wanted to know if you came in here. I told him you did now an' then." She frowned and gazed down her long nose at Larsen. "That's okay, ain't it?"

". . . Sure. Is that all he said?"

"Said he and you would get together, then he left the place."

"What did he look like?"

"Average height, I guess. Husky, with big shoulders. Not exactly fat, though."

"What color hair?"

"Dark. Black, I think. Tell you the truth, I didn't pay much attention. We was awful busy at the time." With her loping gait, she walked quickly behind the counter and returned with an overflowing glass of water. Then she hurried away to get Larsen's order.

After dinner Larsen had two cups of coffee and read about weddings and funerals in the local paper. Then he returned directly to the Clover Motel, locked his cabin door, and began packing for his morning flight to Washington.

Larsen left the motel at 3 A.M. He had to turn in the car at Kennedy and board his plane by seven. He tossed suitcase and vinyl garment bag into the trunk of the rented Chevy, then walked to open the door on the driver's side. Gravel crunching beneath the soles of his shoes sounded amazingly loud in the dark, quiet morning. In the moonlight he saw that the cream-colored car was coated glass and all with a faint film of moisture, like fine white dust that had settled over a period of years, of interest to archaeologists. It seemed impossible that the car would actually start, roll over the brittle gravel and take him away from here.

He unlocked the door and got behind the steering wheel. The car's interior smelled damp, mildewed. It was difficult to see out through the mist on the windshield.

Larsen started the engine and switched on the wipers. A

double arc of clear glass looking out on a vast black sky appeared before him. He put the car into reverse and turned in the seat to back from his parking slot.

Even over the sound of the engine, Larsen could hear the shrill, constant scream of insects coming from the woods near the motel cabin. He drove from the parking lot faster than he intended, causing the car's tires to fling gravel against the inside of the fenders in a mad drumbeat. He glanced at his watch and told himself that he had plenty of time to make his flight.

In the shadows beneath the trees, a square-shouldered, oddly intense figure stood motionless in the tall, damp grass, facing the receding car. The car's twin taillights seemed to draw closer together, then appeared to merge and wink out as the car rounded a distant curve and disappeared. But the figure stood for some time longer, staring fixedly in the same direction.

3

Andrews watched from behind his desk as Judy Carnegie showed Dana Larsen into his office. Larsen cast his kindly, professional charm like lamplight on Judy, who was smiling as she left the two men alone.

"It's good of you to make time to see me," Larsen said, as he and Andrews shook hands. Larsen's hand was moist but cool. As he sat in a chair near Andrews' desk, his eyes took in the veined marble clock on a bookshelf. It was ten fifteen; he was fifteen minutes late for his appointment. "My flight was one of those stacked up at Dulles," he said by way of explanation.

"I'd have waited around," Andrews said casually, to put Larsen at ease. He sensed an uncharacteristic tension in his old friend. "Besides," he added, "I knew it was important, or you wouldn't have made the trip."

For an instant Larsen seemed vaguely embarrassed, as if suddenly doubting the propriety of his visit. "It's about my series of talks with Martin Karpp," he said hesitantly.

"I assumed it would be. How's the research going?"

"Karpp has given me insights that are imperative for any sort of in-depth study of multiple personality. And he talks quite freely, referring to his other selves in the third person and taking our discussions seriously enough. Progress is being made."

"Can I get you a bourbon on the rocks?" Andrews asked.

Larsen looked astounded. "Jesus, Jerry, it's only a little past ten in the morning!"

Andrews grinned. He'd known that Larsen was a teetotaler. But something had been needed to break the shell of "U.S. Senator" around Andrews that he found often kept even long-time friends like Dana Larsen from freely communicating.

Larsen seemed a bit more at ease as he realized he'd been the victim of psychology—his game—and returned Andrews' grin. He removed his dark-rimmed glasses and absently polished the lenses with a wrinkled handkerchief. "You're in the right business, Jerry. It's good that you never continued trying to become an engineer."

"I didn't really want to study engineering," Andrews said. "It was that postgraduate instructor in trig, the one with the great figure. But don't tell my political opponents. We're not supposed to experience those urges."

Larsen said suddenly, "There's something about Karpp—"

Andrews raised a hand palm out, as if in casual self-defense against a thrown object. "Please, Dana, don't tell me you've learned something new and important about the Hugh Drake assassination. A dozen witnesses in that shopping center crowd saw Karpp squeeze the trigger. And the crime's been investigated and reported upon by everybody but the SPCA."

"Of course Karpp's guilty." Larsen seemed irritated now. "It isn't that." Parchment flesh beneath his left eye was drawn nerve-tight as if by thread and needle, causing Andrews' own eyes to water. "I received a written message at my motel last week from Paul Liggett." He paused and stared at Andrews.

Andrews explored his mental file for a face to put with Liggett's name, could come up with none.

"Liggett is one of Karpp's six personalities," Larsen explained.

Andrews remembered then from the relentless media coverage following Karpp's arrest. He sat back in his swivel chair, hearing its faint squeak. Puzzlement always prompted caution in him. That was a prerequisite for political survival. "What sort of message?"

"A warning, strongly suggesting that I leave the Carltonville area."

"Could Karpp somehow have sent it from the asylum?"

"I'm told that's impossible," Larsen said. "I believe it. When Karpp so much as has a bowel movement, it's X-rayed."

Larsen seemed so serious that for a moment Andrews thought he'd meant what he said.

"The note was delivered to the motel desk," Larsen went on. "No one seems to have seen who left it there."

"So it's some local weirdo's attempt at a joke," Andrews suggested.

"I don't think so, Jerry. It disturbed me, because the day before, when I'd come back to my motel cabin after my interview with Karpp, I got the impression that someone had been there in my absence."

"Impression?"

"A general feeling that things weren't exactly as I'd left them. Ashtray a few inches to one side on the desk; suitcase at a slightly different angle on the chair; clothes hanging in the closet where I'd left them, but not quite the way they were on the hangers."

"That could be either imagination or maid service," Andrews said.

"The maid had already been there that morning. And there's more. Yesterday the waitress at the restaurant where I usually ate supper told me someone had been in earlier asking for me. She described Martin Karpp."

"Generally or specifically?"

"Generally," Larsen conceded.

"What does Karpp say about all this?"

"I haven't seen him since I talked to the waitress, but I'm sure his reaction would be much as it was when I asked him about the Paul Liggett message. He wasn't at all surprised that Liggett was active outside the asylum walls. You must remember, to Karpp, Liggett is a separate entity with his own life."

That thought somewhat boggled Andrews' mind. "But the trial made Karpp fully aware of his various personalities."

"Karpp is, to say the least, ambiguous about that. He's an ambiguity in a lot of respects. How much of it is feigned—if any—is difficult to perceive."

Andrews clasped his hands behind his head, leaned farther back in his chair and stared up at the ceiling. There were no answers written on the finely cracked pale plaster; there hadn't been any yet. The swivel chair squealed gratingly as he lowered his gaze and sat forward to rest his elbows on the desk.

"What are you trying to tell me, Dana?" he asked softly. "That one of Karpp's personalities is moving around in flesh and blood form outside the asylum walls and threatening you?"

"I don't know," Larsen said. He nervously adjusted his glasses with a tap of his forefinger at the bridge of his nose. "That's what bothers me. I'm a practical man, a scientist. This seems to go beyond the realm of logical theory, both in what's been happening and in my primal, dominantly emotional reaction to it. That's why I'm concerned, why I'm here."

"What can I do?"

"You can make *sure* there's no possible way Karpp could be slipping out of that asylum."

"Slipping out? My God, Dana, it's a maximum-security federal institution!"

"That's what they say there, Jerry. And I'll admit security's tight. But it isn't like a genuine federal prison."

Andrews tapped a pencil on his desk pad, staring at the faint series of dots the point was leaving. "Do you really think Karpp could be getting out?"

"No."

"But you might be wrong."

Larsen nodded. "It's a world full of variables. And right now I don't know what else to do about the situation." He shifted his weight in his chair, crossing his legs to reveal a pattern of creases from when he'd sat during his flight and through time circling Dulles International. "I thought you ought to know about the matter, unexplainable as it is."

"I'm glad you came," Andrews told him, meaning it.

"I'm not a man who believes in premonitions, not without provable basis, but I have a bad feeling about this."

"I can see that. I'll look into it, Dana, I really will."

Larsen stood, rubbed his hands together as if he were unexpectedly cold. "I know you're busy—"

"The hell with that," Andrews said. "Lunch is open."

"Thanks," Larsen said, "but I've got a flight out at twelve twenty. I made it a turnabout trip so I could get back as soon as possible."

"You're going back? To the asylum?"

"Just for a few more days. I have to finish up. Then I'll go to New York and organize what I've got."

Andrews didn't know exactly what to say. He still wasn't sure in what light he should view Larsen's visit. "I'd be careful —feeling the way you do."

"There's probably nothing to be careful of," Larsen said, but his smile was stiff. "Talking to you has made me feel easier."

"But not foolish, I hope."

"No, not foolish. I had confidence that you'd understand. You inspire that sort of confidence, you know."

"It brings votes," Andrews said. He didn't know himself whether he was joking. "You're right about it being a world of variables. Take care, Dana."

"Always." Larsen shook hands again with Andrews and walked from the office. Andrews heard him chat briefly with Judy Carnegie before leaving.

For a few minutes Andrews sat thinking about what Larsen

had told him. Then Judy knocked lightly on the door and poked her head into the office. "That meeting with the finance committee is in five minutes, Senator."

Good God, five minutes!

Andrews rose from his desk, slipped his coat on and straightened his tie.

"Write me a reminder to talk to someone about the Belmont sanitarium in New York," he said to Judy, as he snatched up his attaché case and hurried from the office. He almost snagged his coattail as he closed the door.

In the press of activities during the remainder of the day, he forgot about Dana Larsen.

4

As Andrews was leaving his office in Washington, in Carltonville, Gabe Beecher, manager of the Chicken Barn restaurant, wearily set his tenth order of the scrambled eggs with diced ham special in front of a waiting customer.

"Where's Carla today?" the customer, a ruddy farmer named French, asked as he salted his eggs.

Gabe wiped his hands on a towel that was tucked in his belt. "Didn't show up this mornin' is all I know."

"Sick, I guess," French said.

Gabe shrugged narrow, muscle-bunched shoulders. "Couldn't say. She ain't called in yet."

Emma, the part-time waitress, smiled a toothy goodbye to the last of the breakfast crowd except for French and walked over to perch on a counter stool. "If you want," she said to Gabe, "I'll run on over to Carla's place and see if she's sick or something. There must be some reason she didn't answer her phone or call in to let you know what was happening." It was obvious from Emma's tone that she hoped Carla's reason wasn't adequate. Carla was Gabe's half sister, but Emma liked to think that business was thicker than blood. And everyone knew that she was a better waitress than Carla, who tended to spill things and act overly secure in her job. What Carla didn't know about was the night Emma had spent with Gabe in Tarrytown.

"Tell you what," Gabe said, pulling the towel from his belt and tossing it onto the counter, "you stay here awhile extra and handle the late customers, and I'll run over to Carla's."

"Sure," Emma said, sliding down off the stool and smoothing her waitress uniform skirt. "Glad to." It might be better that way. Gabe might catch Carla by surprise, before she'd had time to make up some excuse for just plain oversleeping.

Gabe studied Emma as he tucked in his shirt before leaving. In a lot of ways, he regretted that night they had spent together. Emma thought now that she had some sort of permanen claim on him. And it was ugly the way she kept trying to cut up Carla behind her back. Poor, clumsy, gentle-hearted Carla, whose only transgression was that she stood between Emma and where Emma wanted to go. Emma was a problem for Gabe. He wanted her in bed, but not in any other way. But he wanted her in bed badly.

"Back in fifteen minutes," he said, moving to the door.

Emma stuck a pencil into the wave of her butterscotch blond hair and nodded. "You're in good hands," she said. She gave him a smile that meant something.

Gabe jogged across the highway in the backwash of a speeding semi that blasted its air horn at him. He walked about a quarter of a mile, then strode down the grass-inundated lane to the clapboard two-bedroom house with its green-painted foundation. Carla shared the house with another girl, Lila English. But Lila was gone now, visiting a distant relative in Alaska—or so she said. Carla had hinted at a boyfriend in Buffalo.

Gabe stepped up onto the iron-railed plank porch and knocked. He got no answer. He knocked again, waited, then twisted the knob and found the door unlocked.

At that moment Gabe felt a prickle of dreadful certainty whose very lack of foundation scared him. He was sure that something was wrong, unnaturally wrong, inside the house. He couldn't say how he knew, but by all of his faith in God and the Virgin, he knew. He pushed open the door and stepped into the house.

As soon as he was inside, he saw the door to the basement hanging wide open. He was drawn to the darkness beyond the door.

Quiet. Everything was so quiet. Even the floor beneath his feet didn't creak in the slightest.

When Gabe switched on the basement light, he was so positive of what he'd see that he wasn't really surprised.

Carla, clad in her disheveled yellow uniform, lay sprawled at the bottom of the basement stairs. The instant he saw her, Gabe knew she was dead. Her head was turned impossibly far to one side, her eyes open, as if over her shoulder she were surveying in alarm the jagged run in the panty hose on her long, exposed leg.

"Carla!" Gabe called instinctively. Then, knowing she was dead, he stepped back in the irrational fear that she might answer. The fear bored its way into the pit of his stomach and made him nauseated and dizzy.

For a long time he stood gazing down the sloping tunnel of the stairwell. At the other end, Death seemed to have created a dark vacuum, gently, somehow enticingly, drawing him. The perfect stillness of Carla amazed and fascinated.

Gabe backed away slowly, pausing between steps, gaining strength with distance. He turned and made his way to the phone on the table in the tiny entrance hall and awkwardly dialed the first number he could think of, the restaurant number. Emma answered.

"I ain't gonna be back for a while," Gabe told her. "And I ain't feelin' so well. You do me a favor, will you, and phone the law and send them on over to Carla's place?"

"Sure," Emma said, sounding surprised and curious. "What's Carla done now?"

Gabe leaned weakly against the wall and stared out the door at the brightness of the sun on green shrubbery. Over and over in his mind, Carla was stumbling and pitching headfirst down the basement stairs, frightened and screaming.

"What Carla's done," he told Emma, "is had herself a fatal accident."

He was vaguely aware of Emma hanging up.

5

A week later, at ten o'clock on an unpredictably gusty evening, Andrews parked his car on Hyde Boulevard and walked a few blocks farther to the Adelaire Hotel. The night was cool, and it was beginning to drizzle, forming dark, wind-rippled puddles and spotting Andrews' lined raincoat. Sewer grates steamed with the unexpected warmth.

The neighborhood once had been one of Washington's better areas, had declined and now was being revitalized by fresh federal funding and construction. The buildings were old, many of them Georgian, and lately had acquired a refurbished colonial charm that mixed curiously with the angular new construction on the street.

A traffic light in the next block changed to green, and half a dozen cars swished past on the wet street like intense caged animals suddenly released. Andrews brushed the rain from his hair and began unbuttoning his coat as he stepped into the Adelaire's lobby.

The hotel was one of the older ones that recently had been redecorated. It was a good, even a plush, hotel, but still not regularly frequented by the real movers and shakers, the politicos of the city. It was where Andrews could be certain of privacy whenever Pat Colombo came into Washington to see him.

There were quite a few people in the opulently furnished

blue-carpeted lobby, most of them probably tourists, none of them familiar to Andrews. He walked past the entrance to the small, dim lounge and crossed to the elevators. Pat had given him her room number when she'd phoned that afternoon.

There was no one in the hall when he knocked. She opened the door immediately and smiled at him. After he kissed her, she suggested that he close the door and take off his coat.

"It's raining out there," Andrews told her, unnecessarily. He always was at an initial loss for meaningful words when they met.

"It doesn't matter what's happening outside," she said.

Pat Colombo was a dark-eyed brunette with a short, fetchingly ten pounds overweight figure and a smile straight out of Italian Renaissance art. Her features were classic and serene, but her real beauty lay in her gracefulness and her seeming unawareness of self. They both knew that she was not at all like Ellen.

Two years ago Pat had been one of the aides to Senator Jack Zale, and had been assigned by Zale to work with Andrews in organizing the opposition to an accelerated arms-race bill. They had worked closely for months, and Pat had sensed Andrews' problems with Ellen. But it was Andrews who had made the abrupt and unplanned advance that resulted in their becoming lovers. He'd never regretted it.

On the table before the suite's sofa was a scotch and water waiting for Andrews. A half-full wineglass was beside it. Andrews draped his wet raincoat over the back of a vinyl chair and picked up his drink. It was hardly diluted; she must have just mixed it.

"Tough week?" she asked, posing the question almost like a suburban housewife asking her husband if he'd had a hard day. She brushed past him, picked up her wine and sat down on the sofa.

"A busy week," he said.

"But you love your work."

"Do I?"

"Too strong a word, love?"

"I don't know yet. Politics is like scuba diving. The deeper you get, the more pressure comes to bear."

Pat's dark eyes appraised him as she sipped her drink. "I'd have thought you'd regard your progress as getting higher rather than deeper."

"Maybe I should." He sat next to her, near her. "Each day in office, power becomes a more recognizable currency: favors owed, favors paid. If you're not careful, the balance of one to the other becomes the object of the game."

"You've just described politics in the proverbial nutshell," Pat told him. "But isn't the important thing how you use that accumulated power?"

"The important thing is what's backing up that power as currency. Is it the will of your constituents or the fear of your peers?"

"It sounds complicated enough to provide plenty of convenient outs," Pat observed.

Andrews laughed and pulled her to him, kissing her again and feeling himself drawn toward her calm and mysterious center. She spilled the rest of her wine, splashing some of it onto her dress. Ellen would have leaped up, screaming her indignation, calculatingly choosing words to further wound their already maimed marriage.

Pat said nothing as Andrews released her. Then she suddenly clung to him, working her fingertips into his back as if reassuring herself of his presence. He carried her to the bed, as he often did jokingly, but this time he didn't laugh and she didn't do her usual exaggerated swoon.

Pat Colombo approached sex as she did everything else, directly and honestly. A need recognized and filled, a giving and sharing without implications. As Andrews held her more tightly and thrust himself into her with increasing intensity, she seemed to encourage him with her own compounding passion, her lush body writhing and contracting beneath him as if straining to give birth to their relief and renewal.

When Andrews withdrew from her, lay breathing deeply beside her, she rested a weightless hand on his arm. Someone ran water in the room above or alongside theirs, and Andrews could hear and feel the flow of it through the pipes within the walls. For a moment he felt as if he and Pat were within some protective massive organism, with copper pipes, air conditioning and heating ducts for arteries, electrical wiring for some bizarre nervous system. Then, with a squeal and a rattle, the flow of water ceased. From outside, six stories below, came the angry sound of a car horn blasting several times in rapid succession.

"The Senate recesses for three weeks after next Thursday," Andrews said. He felt the mattress shift as Pat stirred beside him. "Why don't we go to the cabin for that last week?"

Andrews and Pat had spent time at the cabin before. It was a small, modern and very secluded structure in the mountains of Colorado. Shortly after meeting Pat, Andrews had bought the cabin through a straw party and had it refurbished. It was equipped with a furnace and air conditioner, kitchen facilities and a telephone that had never once rung. Everything he and Pat needed was there.

"I'll let you know if I can get away from work," Pat said. She was an editor for a national financial magazine headquartered in Boulder, Colorado. "You know I'll try."

"I could use a week of quiet and sanity."

"I'd settle for just one of the two," Pat remarked drowsily.

Andrews raised his upper body, supporting himself on the mattress with his elbows. "Dammit," he muttered.

Pat rearranged her hair and turned to look at him. "What's the matter?"

He said, "I just remembered something I forgot to do."

Dr. Dana Larsen sat in his office in his West Fifty-seventh

Street Manhattan condominium and gave the rough schedule on his desk a last quick check. It was here in New York that Martin Karpp had through his six identities pursued what were in effect six different lives. Each of these identities had been shallowly explored for sensationalism by the news media immediately following Karpp's confinement. And defense psychiatrists had delved into the lives of these identities only deeply enough to establish legally that they did indeed exist, each in the body of Martin Karpp. But Larsen would be the first to study thoroughly and scientifically the splintered pasts of Karpp's five other personalities.

He was excited by the prospect. Court transcripts had provided him with several leads, as had his conversations with Karpp. It wouldn't be difficult to contact people who had known the various Karpps by their pseudonyms, not suspecting that their acquaintance was at times different people entirely in every way but physical. How these lives interrelated was what interested Larsen.

The cloying uneasiness that had gripped him in Carltonville had all but disappeared. There was much still unexplainable about what had happened there, but it was the more immediate and important unexplainable that now compelled Larsen. He regretted his visit with Jerry Andrews. But at least he could depend on Jerry not ever to remind him or anyone else of those unreasonable and inexact fears. Jerry Andrews always had recognized and respected the various needs and apprehensions in people, which was why he was such a successful politician.

Though it was well past midnight, lighted windows still sequined the night beyond the sliding glass doors opening onto Larsen's small balcony. Larsen got up from his desk and stretched elaborately, then walked out onto the balcony and breathed in the cold night air. A dozen stories below, a few pedestrians scurried like nocturnal insects on the sidewalk, and a tiny, foreshortened cab veered to the building's entrance to deliver a passenger. Larsen wasn't tired and knew he wouldn't be able to relax fully until he'd completed the second phase of his research on Karpp.

Though he'd already begun that phase, it occurred to him that some of the places he needed to visit, some of the people he needed to talk with, would be most accessible in the late night hours. Why not continue his investigation now—tonight?

The idea gained appeal for Larsen. It would be more interesting than a glass of milk and a few hours of scrap-time TV, and undoubtedly more productive. So enthusiastic was he that he didn't realize he was shivering from the cold.

He returned to his desk, copied a name and address on a slip of paper which he stuffed into his shirt pocket, then shrugged into his brown sport jacket and topcoat. After placing his precious notes in a safe place and locking the door behind him carefully—there had been three break-ins in the building during his absence—he took the elevator down to the basement garage where his car was parked.

Larsen turned left on Fifty-seventh and headed for Broadway and Columbus Circle. There was comparatively little traffic on the streets, and few pedestrians. A young couple walking arm in arm stepped gingerly around a ragged figure slumped against a building and tenaciously clutching a brown-bagged bottle. The girl was wearing a long dress that swept the pavement, and her escort had on a dark suit and black tie. The pathetic figure at their feet didn't move. Manhattan's mad juxtaposition of ugliness and beauty, wealth and poverty, never failed to intrigue Larsen.

He was making a left turn onto Eighth Avenue to get onto Broadway when he glanced in his rear-view mirror.

A pair of flat dark eyes stared back at him from the rear seat.

6

Judy Carnegie stood in the doorway to Andrews' office wearing an expression between puzzlement and dismay. Andrews glanced up at her, waiting for her to speak, then did a double take when he saw her face.

"You all right, Jude?"

"I phoned Belmont sanitarium," she said. "Your friend Dr. Larsen, he's dead . . ."

Andrews felt that dark sinking sensation he'd felt before on learning of the death of an old friend, on being reminded that time was demanding its due. He had known Dana Larsen when Dana still was bothered by youthful acne, then when he had become "Dr." Dana Larsen, and now Dana would become a name and date chiseled on cold stone.

"What happened to him?" Andrews asked.

Judy gave a vague shrug. "His body was found in New York, in the Hudson River."

"When?"

"Yesterday. They said at the sanitarium that he'd drowned, but they didn't know much else about it."

Andrews sat silently for a moment. Dana Larsen dead by drowning. That, of all things, struck with heavy irony. Andrews remembered Dana stroking through the sun-shot waters of Lake Michigan on a long-ago summer vacation, pulling in the small boy who had become separated from his rubber raft in the wind-roughened, surprisingly powerful surf. Dana had reached the floundering boy within minutes, placed him back on the raft and effortlessly propelled him to shore. And Dana had been wearing pants and shirt.

It was meaningless to speculate without facts, Andrews cautioned himself. "Get me a *New York Times*," he said to Judy, who nodded and disappeared.

The *Times* account of Dana's death shed little added light. His body had been spotted by a cabdriver in the early morning floating in the Hudson near Manhattan's lower West Side. The corpse apparently hadn't been in the water long. Dana was identified by some plastic credit cards in his wallet, which also contained sixty-seven dollars, and transported to the city morgue. At this time, the police had no reason to suspect foul play.

Andrews tossed the folded paper onto a desk corner, walked thoughtfully to the small bar in the office and poured himself three fingers of scotch.

No reason to suspect foul play, he repeated to himself. Yet Dana had felt threatened. That was why he had come to Andrews. And Andrews had, in the press of more "important" matters, done nothing until this morning—when it was too late.

Half the scotch in Andrews' glass disappeared in one gulp.

Judy knocked on the door, tentatively opened it and peered inside. She was her practical and calculating self again. When she saw the glass of liquor in Andrews' hand, her dark eyes barely registered the fact. Her voice was its usual crisp instrument of efficiency. "Senator, you have the meeting with Bethancourt and Hallock in ten minutes."

Andrews stared into the amber prism of his drink and nodded. "Thanks, Judy."

When she'd left him alone again, he went back to his desk and sat down. He thumbed through his telephone index to find a name he had almost forgotten. The name belonged to a captain on the New York Police Department who had been a friend of Andrews' father. The captain, Amos Franks, had known Andrews casually since childhood, though they hadn't seen each other in over five years.

Andrews didn't locate Franks' name in his desk index. He pressed an intercom button. "Judy, call Hallock and tell him I'll be about twenty minutes late. Then get the New York Police Department and see if you can run down a Captain Amos Franks for me."

Within ten minutes, Franks was on the phone.

"Senator Andrews, it's been a while. How are you?"

At the sound of the deep, mellow voice, the image of Franks became vivid in Andrews' mind. Amos Franks was a huge black man, ugly, amiable and tough. And smart. "I'm fine, Amos. Yourself?"

"As ever. I've been reading good things about your work down in Washington."

"You know how it is, Amos. The media is always with you until you screw up."

Deep laughter rumbled over the line. "Isn't that just the truth!"

"I need to know a few things, Amos. About a Dr. Dana Larsen. His body was found yesterday in the Hudson."

"I know the case but not the details. What sort of information do you need?"

"Whatever's available. Maybe some that isn't. Larsen was a close friend of mine, Amos."

"Hm . . . Let me get back to you, Senator. Say an hour?"

"It'll have to be an hour and a half, Amos. I've got a meeting that's a must." Andrews gave Franks his number and told him Judy would put his call through immediately.

At the meeting with Hallock and Bethancourt, Hallock asked Andrews several times if something was bothering him. The old senator was shrewd enough to know when not to push, and apparently he decided that whatever pressure he and the adamant Bethancourt were going to bring to bear should be applied at another time.

The meeting ended prematurely with Hallock urging Andrews to reconsider his vote on the water appropriations bill during the coming recess. Andrews assured the senator that he would, though he couldn't envision himself changing his mind until the President changed those deceptive and costly amendments. And Andrews wasn't the only dissenter who held that opinion, so a compromise might be reached. Always a compromise.

Amos Franks called back exactly on schedule.

"Not much to tell you, Senator," he said regretfully.

Andrews searched Franks' voice for any sign of hesitancy. So many people still had reservations about being candid on the phone. The vestiges of Watergate.

"Anything is more than what I have, Amos," Andrews said.

"The deceased was spotted in the Hudson River at six-oh-three yesterday morning by Edward Mariquan, a cabdriver who'd just dropped a fare nearby. Mariquan phoned us and we responded by patrol car. The deceased was drowned, according to the autopsy just conducted. He'd also received a blow on the head hard enough to fracture the skull."

Andrews felt his stomach lurch. "Received a blow before or after drowning?"

"Before."

"But . . . Wouldn't that mean . . . ?"

"Not necessarily, Senator. He must have fallen into the water, and chances are he was knocked unconscious and couldn't save himself. Most of the stiffs—bodies—we fish from the river have injuries sustained before death."

"Were there any other wounds on the body?"

"That was the extent of it," Franks said. "It's going down as accidental death."

"That's on the official records," Andrews said. "How is it going down with you, Amos?"

There was a pause. "Now, Senator . . ."

"I understand your position, Amos."

"Do you? It's not my job to speculate irresponsibly, or to buck the record unless I have some cause, some sort of evidence."

"I'm not asking you not to do your job," Andrews said. "And what you say will be off the record—off any kind of record."

"I can't tell you he was murdered, Senator. And I can't tell you he wasn't."

"I want a guess."

"I can't make a guess, can't give you percentages. We find a man with a cracked skull and water in his lungs. No other injuries, no apparent robbery. We make a preliminary investigation, then go on to other things. We've got no choice. Sure, Senator, your friend might have been murdered. He might have been killed by a mugger that panicked and didn't take his money or jewelry. Or our preliminary might turn up somebody with a strong motive that bears further investigation. But I'll be honest, Senator. Odds are, it ends right here."

"Will you do me a favor, Amos? Call me if anything else turns up?"

"Sure." The tone of Franks' voice indicated that he was going to say something more. "You understand, sir, we find hundreds of people every year who might have been murdered. It's not like in the detective novels. Sometimes people kill for reasons so petty they don't register as motives, sometimes for no reason at all. Those kinds of killings are like when lightning strikes. Nobody can predict them, prevent them or do anything about them after they occur. The thing is to accept them and go on to matters we can do something about, because we don't have any alternative."

"I understand, Amos. Thanks."

Andrews hung up the phone and realized that his muscles were rigid from the tension of his conversation. He settled into his desk chair and made himself relax. Maybe he should have told Franks about the message left at Dana Larsen's motel in Carltonville, about Dana's suspicion that someone had searched his cabin in his absence. But that was nothing, Andrews knew. A practical joke, an unfounded, unreported assumption. Nothing. Unless you had known Dana Larsen for the unflappable realist that he was, and had witnessed his uncharacteristic uneasiness when he'd told his story.

Andrews' intercom buzzed, startling him.

"Senator," Judy's voice said briskly, "Mrs. Hopperman of the Highway Beautification League is here."

Andrews stood up from behind his desk and left his office to usher in Mrs. Hopperman personally, launching himself on the business of the day.

But he didn't completely forget about Dana Larsen. Not this time.

7

"I'm going to have to take a business trip during the coming adjournment," Andrews told his wife that evening in the brick-walled den of their Williamsburg home.

"Are you?" Ellen said with disinterest that almost dripped. She was sitting in the flickering glow emanating from the flames behind the glass fire screen that protected the glossy hardwood floor from sparks. Her shapely legs were propped up somehow insolently on a hassock, and she was idly leafing through what appeared to be a catalog of expensive jewelry. Ellen had a weakness for jewelry.

At forty, she appeared ten years younger, slim of waist and hip, gaunt of chest. Her shoulders were slightly stooped. Her face, with its prominent cheekbones and sweeping, lean jaw line, would have possessed a sought-after fashion-model look but for her nose, which was turned up and jauntily incongruous on such an otherwise hungry countenance. When she was younger, Ellen couldn't leave men alone. Now she could but didn't. Love had changed to indifference in Ellen. Sex remained. But not with Andrews.

"You'll be here?" he asked.

"No," she said. Her heavily made-up gray eyes didn't flicker as she flipped a colorful page of whatever she was reading.

Andrews didn't ask where she'd be, though he didn't doubt it would be with Millikin. In that respect he trusted her to be discreet, because if her longtime affair with Millikin, a lawyer who had handled Andrews' father's estate, became public knowledge, Andrews could divorce her without any more political damage than had been done. And Ellen wanted above all to maintain her position and wealth as Andrews' wife.

As for Andrews, he could accept their situation. They weren't the first political couple to continue a marriage publicly because neither would stand to gain from a divorce. Through the years they had learned to make room for each other, to lead separate, private lives. In the beginning, Andrews had thought that their arrangement couldn't go on for very long, but it had. There simply was no real reason to end it. They had adapted.

The root of their situation was easy enough to identify for Andrews. Six years ago Ellen had married him for money and status. Nothing complex about it. Since then she had no longer liked herself or Andrews. Possibly she hadn't foreseen that.

Andrews had been almost glad when two years ago she had taken up with the unctuous and worldwise Lawrence Millikin. Like Ellen, he understood the situation and would be discreet.

Shortly thereafter, Andrews had met Pat Colombo. She became the fourth person other than Andrews to know and understand his position. Judy Carnegie had been the third. From the beginning, Andrews knew it would be stupid to try to keep that sort of secret from Judy.

The applecart continued to roll and not be upset. In fact, not an apple had dropped.

"A friend of yours died," Ellen said unexpectedly, flipping another glossy page.

"Dana Larsen," Andrews said. He looked closely at her impassive, fire-shadowed features. "How did you know?"

"Kate Hogan happened to phone me from New York. It was in the papers there." She turned to focus artfully slanted eyes on Andrews. "But how on earth did you find out so soon?"

"Somewhat the way you did," Andrews said.

"An unfortunate accident." She returned her attention to her reading.

Andrews said nothing more. He got up from his deep armchair and left the room, feeling the coolness of Ellen recede as he went into the kitchen. He considered having a scotch, then decided against it and poured himself a glass of milk. He often awoke in the middle of the night if he tried to unwind near bedtime with alcohol.

He tossed down the milk, rinsed the glass and climbed the stairs to his bedroom at the end of the second-floor hall.

Andrews' bedroom was spacious and carpeted in pale green. Within reach of the king-size bed were a bookcase and a table on which sat a digital clock-radio with a built-on reading lamp. The bed's headboard was brass. The rest of the furniture was walnut and there was not much of it. The effect was tasteful and restful. On one wall was an oil painting of the Irish seacoast. The painting had been given to Andrews years ago by a friend he'd endorsed for an unsuccessful Senate race. It wasn't a particularly good painting, but its colors matched the décor, so he left it. On another wall was a studio photograph of Andrews' father, taken when he was in his late thirties, slightly younger than Andrews' age now. Occasionally, as he lay in bed before sleep, that fact amazed and frightened Andrews.

Before undressing, Andrews switched on the portable Sony TV. An old movie came on the screen, a Western. A beautiful woman in a long dress—maybe Joan Blondell—was arguing with Randolph Scott. Suddenly Scott stopped arguing and grabbed her and kissed her. She fought with spirit at first, then returned the kiss with equal enthusiasm. An arrow abruptly fixed itself in the wooden buckboard behind them,

/ 49

and Scott threw the woman to the ground to protect her.

Andrews wondered if the real Randolph Scott and Joan Blondell had been even a little bit like their screen counterparts. Or did that matter, as long as we could see some of the best in ourselves in them? Scott was kissing Blondell again, this time with gentle reassurance.

Tomorrow, after the Senate adjournment, Andrews would see if Pat Colombo had found out if she could get away from her work to spend the final week of the three-week recess with him at the Colorado cabin. Andrews would use at least part of the preceding two weeks to look into Dana Larsen's death, for which he felt partly responsible. Moral obligation.

No, Andrews thought, sitting down to remove his shoes and socks, not moral obligation. Nothing so noble. How could he owe anything to Larsen now? What difference could it make to the dead?

Curiosity, then? Something that simple? He stood and took off his shirt. A sense of adventure? A puzzling out of the bizarre for answers with possibly greater implications than anyone anticipated?

Bullshit! Andrews told himself. He walked into the bathroom to brush his teeth.

Moral obligation, he decided, almost with embarrassment.

Shots rang out from the TV.

8

Dr. Laidelier, director of the Belmont sanitarium, led Andrews down a wide hall from the reception area to his office. The doctor was a tall, shambling man with bushy gray eyebrows. He had deep-set blue eyes with diamond glitters of intelligence in them. His gray pinstripe suit, though obviously expensive, hung gracelessly on his long, gangly frame, and Andrews noticed that he was wearing scuffed brown wingtip shoes.

Holding the office door open for Andrews, Dr. Laidelier smiled warmly and motioned for him to enter.

The office was large, well furnished though not plush. One wall was lined with bookshelves that were stuffed with old as well as new volumes packed in with disregard for their arrangement. Along another wall were banks of black file cabinets. Behind the doctor's unpretentious metal desk was a wide window overlooking the sanitarium grounds.

"You told my secretary that this was about Martin Karpp, Senator," Dr. Laidelier said, lowering his tall frame in sections into the chair behind the desk.

Andrews was seated in an upholstered chair that undoubtedly was more comfortable than Laidelier's desk chair. He wondered if the office's effects were carefully calculated for the benefit of the patients. "About Martin Karpp," Andrews said, "and about Dr. Dana Larsen."

"A tragic thing about Dr. Larsen," Laidelier said. He sounded sincere. He was a man who projected sincerity to spare.

"Did Dr. Larsen discuss his work concerning Karpp with you?" Andrews asked.

Laidelier shook his head no. "He came and he went. We talked a few times about things in general, but not about Karpp or Dr. Larsen's work."

"Then he never came to you and questioned the security surrounding Karpp?"

Laidelier's vivid eyes caught the angled sun and deflected it in Andrews' direction. "I don't understand what you mean . . . security. I assure you that Karpp is well guarded."

"It's the possibility of his escape that concerned Dr. Larsen," Andrews said.

The tall, unkempt man behind the desk was silent as he carefully regarded Andrews. He was one of the few men whose scrutiny made Andrews vaguely uncomfortable and produced the compulsion to squirm in his chair. But Andrews sat still.

"It would probably be a good idea, Senator," Laidelier said, "if I called Joseph Morgan in here. He's chief of security at Belmont."

Andrews nodded, and Laidelier pressed an intercom button and asked his secretary to summon Joseph Morgan.

Within a few minutes Joseph Morgan was seated in a chair near the opposite corner of Laidelier's desk, so that the three men formed a perfectly equilateral triangle. Morgan was a beefy, well-dressed man with reddish-blond straight hair and the moon face of a saddened choirboy. He sat totally relaxed and looked with frank curiosity at Andrews. Morgan hadn't seemed impressed when the doctor introduced him to a U.S. senator. There had been no flicker of the awe or respect Andrews had noted in other lower-echelon government employees. And Morgan did work for the U.S. Government. Dr. Laidelier was in charge of treating the inmates; Morgan was in charge of keeping certain of them here to treat.

"I feel compelled to check on something Dr. Larsen came to me about not long before he died," Andrews said. He looked at Morgan. "Is there any possibility that Martin Karpp could ever have left the asylum, then returned?"

To Morgan's credit, he didn't laugh or put on an incredulous expression. "Not in my estimation, Senator. The asylum's security is tight. The main building, where Karpp is confined, is guarded around the clock and would be escape-proof even without guards. Brick walls, pickproof locks, barred windows. And you've seen the twelve-foot-high brick wall that surrounds the asylum. That wall is ivy-covered and pretty, but it's topped with detection devices so that nothing can come or go over it without us knowing. Beyond the wall and the regular guards are two high, barbed-wire-topped chain-link fences, and the ground between wall and fences is regularly patrolled by guards with trained dobermans."

Dr. Laidelier cleared his throat. "None of that is as noticeable as it might be. We don't treat only the criminally insane here, Senator. Though we pride ourselves on our security system, it has to remain relatively unobtrusive to most of our patients and to their families."

"Karpp is top security," Morgan said. "Someone checks him every few hours." Lightly, yet with great emphasis, Morgan raised a pale hand and tapped the arm of his chair. "Since the time Karpp was placed here, he's been here."

"Mr. Morgan will be glad to let you personally examine our security system," Dr. Laidelier said. He seemed eager for this to happen.

Andrews thanked him, then asked, "Is Martin Karpp receiving any sort of treatment?"

For the first time Laidelier seemed a bit uncomfortable. He spread his long-fingered hands palms down in a gesture of helplessness. "Not to the degree I'd like," he said. "We have only so much staff, so much operating capital. And frankly,

Martin Karpp is here for life anyway, so we concentrate more on patients who have a chance for recovery and functional lives in outside society. Or who are under severe stress or in agony, which also doesn't apply to Karpp. Priorities. Seemingly harsh. But realistic, I'm afraid."

"I understand the realities," Andrews said.

Dr. Laidelier smiled, as if to agree that, yes, a successful politician would. It was the first move he'd made that Andrews didn't like. Beyond the doctor, outside the wide window, greenish-brown lawn stretched away in a mild slope to the vine-patterned brick wall. A line of small trees stood in grassless, geometrically perfect circles, their lower trunks painted antiseptic white. There were a few low shrubs here and there, and several ornate concrete benches. Off to the left was something that looked like a gazebo. All in all, a tranquil scene.

Almost impulsively, Andrews said, "I'd like to talk to Martin Karpp."

"That's easy enough to arrange," Laidelier said amicably.

Andrews stood, offered his hand. "I don't want to take up any more of your time, Doctor. Your help's appreciated."

Dr. Laidelier stood with a curious unfolding motion and shook hands. "Would you like Mr. Morgan to give you a tour of the grounds before or after you talk with Karpp?"

"It really doesn't matter."

"We can go now, then," Morgan said. Dr. Laidelier's authority over him apparently was limited if well defined. "After you, Senator."

But at the door, Dr. Laidelier's voice stopped them.

"Just out of curiosity, Senator, why did Dr. Larsen question our security?"

"He came across some evidence suggesting that Martin Karpp was seen outside the asylum walls." Andrews felt it wise not to carry his explanation further.

Dr. Laidelier seemed taken aback. His bushy eyebrows

writhed like caterpillars suffering in unison. "No," he said, "no, that's quite impossible, I assure you."

"Dr. Larsen was such a realist," Andrews said, "even a cynic."

"He was a personal friend?"

"Yes. That's why I want to satisfy my curiosity. Or I suppose what was his curiosity. I feel I owe his memory that much."

"I understand, Senator."

Andrews didn't see how that was possible. *He* didn't actually understand what he was doing here. He left the office and fell in beside Morgan for his tour of the Belmont sanitarium.

The security system was as tight as Dr. Laidelier and Morgan had described it. The buildings themselves were arranged so that the patients' quarters were under constant observation, and all outside doors and windows were kept locked. The high brick wall surrounding the main building and its two smaller counterparts seemed, despite the sparse ivy, unscalable, and it too was built along flat ground that afforded easy viewing and little potential shelter. A number of men strolling about the grounds, whom Andrews had assumed were patients or visiting relatives, turned out to be highly trained armed guards.

But the real security was outside the brick wall, in the half-mile-wide perimeter along the barbed-wire-topped fences that were mostly concealed by woods. There uniformed guards roamed with leashed dogs, and along natural paths photoelectric detectors were set to reveal the passage of anyone who didn't belong in the area. The armed guards had a businesslike, grim air about them. Andrews could understand why Dr. Laidelier preferred that they be kept out of sight of the patients and visitors.

"That's about it, Senator," Morgan said, as they trudged up the blacktop road toward the main building. The security chief was breathing hard from the exertion of the tour, his breath fogging ahead of him in the clear, cool air.

"Seems tight as possible," Andrews said in a deliberately complimentary tone.

"It is, sir." Morgan sounded pleased and proud. "The idea that anyone could have come and gone here without us knowing is—well, it just doesn't wash with me."

"I was never questioning your professionalism," Andrews assured him.

"Oh, I know that, Senator. Do you want to talk with Karpp now or later?"

"Now, if it can be arranged."

Morgan quickened his pace. "It can be arranged."

The room was oddly shaped and gray. Martin Karpp sat across from Andrews, his bulky forearms resting on the oak table between them. Behind Karpp was a wall the upper half of which was clear Plexiglas. A guard in a dark-blue business suit stood in the anteroom beyond the transparent partition. He watched Andrews and Karpp with seeming nonchalance and disinterest, but there was a subtle attitude of alertness in his loose stance.

"They told me about Dr. Larsen," Karpp said in a formal, carefully modulated voice. "I'm sorry. I liked him."

Andrews got the impression that Karpp really had been fond of Dana Larsen. The series of interviews was the only real outside human contact Karpp had experienced in years.

"Dr. Larsen told me about a note someone left for him at his motel," Andrews said. "Someone pretending to be you."

Karpp's taut lips lifted in what was only the suggestion of a smile. "Not me, Paul Liggett."

"Aren't you and Paul Liggett one and the same?"

"Yes and no."

"Did Paul Liggett leave the message at the motel?"

Karpp said nothing.

"Do you always remember what Paul Liggett does, Martin?"

"Some of the time. Other times it's just a blank space in my life."

"Then it's possible that Paul Liggett acted without your knowledge."

Karpp seemed irritated by Andrews' inability to grasp. "Of course it's possible."

Andrews sat for a moment studying the stocky, brooding man across the table from him. There was about Karpp a hint of underlying great strength, of awesome will. Andrews felt an iciness run through him, and he almost shivered. In his way, Karpp was more of a shaper of history than Andrews probably ever would be. In his own dark way.

"I remember you from when you were a governor," Karpp said suddenly.

And Andrews realized that circumstances might well have placed him rather than Hugh Drake in Karpp's gunsight. Andrews or anyone else in public life might be a target for someone like Karpp. That, really, was the horror of it.

"Are you all right, Senator?" Karpp asked.

It struck Andrews as ludicrous that Martin Karpp, a certified mental case incarcerated for life, should ask him that. He nodded, then asked, "Martin, how do you feel about being locked up in here?"

"I've thought about it," Karpp said. "I suppose fate is why I'm here, why Jay shot Governor Drake, why I was the one who was caught. Fate all the way down the line."

"Then you accept it?"

"I do, yes."

"And the . . . others?"

Karpp smiled. "It isn't unanimous. But what difference does it make?"

Andrews slowly stood up, nodded to the guard. "I suppose none. Goodbye, Martin. Thanks for talking with me."

"I'll be seeing you, Senator," Martin Karpp said behind Andrews, in a voice that might not have been exactly the voice he'd used a few minutes earlier.

9

Andrews didn't want to risk a breaking-and-entering charge, so he went to see Captain Amos Franks immediately after checking into his New York hotel. Franks hadn't been keen on Andrews snooping about, but he was either too considerate or too wise to try to prevent it. With barely concealed reluctance, he'd given Andrews a key to Dana Larsen's apartment. There was something in Franks' demeanor that suggested to Andrews that he wouldn't have turned over the key if the case had been anything but a virtually closed file.

Larsen had lived alone in a condominium unit on the twentieth floor of a West Fifty-seventh Street building not quite plush enough to employ a doorman. When Andrews pushed on the door, it swung open stiffly onto stale air and unmistakable emptiness. It was as if the possessions of the dead had taken on the peculiar blankness of the dead. The shelves of books and knickknacks, the tables, chairs, opaque-screened TV—all seemed to be nonfunctional museum pieces, for observation only. Maybe what gave that impression was the faint layer of almost imperceptible dust over everything. Maybe it was something else.

Andrews stepped inside and closed the door.

For a while he simply wandered from room to room, getting the feel of the place, trying without realizing it to put himself back in time, in Dana Larsen's shoes.

But there was no real key to the man here, or to the life that he had led. Only a morbid quietude. A distant uncle in Ohio was to arrange for the removal of Dana's effects, Franks had said. The police had made their cursory examination; other than that, everything in the apartment was as Dana had left it, expecting to return to sit down, to walk about, to work, to eat, to watch TV, to sleep, to wake.

One of the two bedrooms had been converted into an office. Andrews entered the room, glanced about at glass-fronted bookcases, a gray file cabinet, a fancy mahogany desk with ball-and-claw feet, a low table with a portable electric typewriter on it. By the Touch-Tone white desk phone was an automatic answering device. Andrews sat down at the desk and played the tape, but no one had left a message for Dana.

Andrews sat back. Was that normal? Surely the police had investigated the answering device, and they seemed to consider it so. But at least some of Dana's old calls should be on the tape.

Then Andrews reminded himself that Dana had been away from home for quite a while before his death. Possibly his acquaintances in the city didn't realize he was back. Or it was possible that he had been there to answer whatever calls had come in and seldom used the answering device. It wasn't activated now, as a matter of fact.

Andrews began to go through Dana's desk. He found only the expected papers, receipts and unpaid bills, along with some notes and a first-draft typed bibliography on the multiple personality phenomenon. There was nothing on Martin Karpp.

After replacing things as they were in the desk drawers, Andrews got up and walked to the filing cabinet near the window. He was glad to find that Dana had arranged things alphabetically. Under "Multiple Personality" were several file folders, also arranged alphabetically. Andrews leafed through the index tabs to "K." There was no file for Martin Karpp.

Andrews slid the file drawer shut on its smooth casters and

stood staring out the window, down at the stream of early-evening, miniaturized Manhattan traffic. The rushing, horn-punctuated sound of the ritualistic turmoil wafted up to him. On the opposite side of the street two men had hurried for the same empty cab and now stood apparently arguing. The cab pulled away and left them both standing. From his observation point, it was impossible for Andrews to judge their reaction.

Almost as impossible as it was for him to try to judge Dana's past actions and reactions.

Then Andrews remembered the brief span of long-ago time when he and Dana had roomed together in college. And he remembered where Dana had put those few things he especially wanted withheld from prying eyes.

In the office closet Andrews found the set of golf clubs. In college, the golf bag had been a tattered canvas affair. This bag was of two-tone blue vinyl. But like the old one, it would be too bulky, unconcealable and obviously inexpensive to interest a sneak thief.

Andrews wrestled the bag from the closet and removed the clubs. There was a honeycombed plastic surface near the mouth of the bag that kept the club shafts separated. Andrews hooked his fingers through two of the holes and pulled until the separator slid out. Then he turned the empty golf bag upside down.

Dana's notes on Martin Karpp fell out onto the carpet.

Andrews stayed in Dana Larsen's office well past suppertime, reading about Martin Karpp. Some of the material was familiar, publicized as soon as the media had dug into Karpp's background immediately after Hugh Drake's murder. Andrews read again about the death of Karpp's parents in an auto accident when he was an infant, then the orphanage when he was two, followed by the inhuman sexually brutal treatment given him by his foster parents, who finally were prosecuted. But not until Martin Karpp, writhing and helpless physically and mentally, finding no escape outward, had escaped inward.

At first Karpp had experienced what he thought of as blackouts, until the evidence of his other selves became overwhelming even to him. Then those other selves intruded into his consciousness, took on individuality and substance there. By the time he was eighteen he came to know them, accept them, the various splintered refugees from himself, of himself.

They had names. There was Alan Hobson, who stole. Willy Bennet, who sometimes thought he was a woman. L. C. Chambers, successful businessman and big spender who had run up debts all over Manhattan. Paul Liggett, in many ways the most real of Karpp's involuntarily fabricated identities. And of course Jay Jefferson, social conscience and political firebrand who had slain a potential president. All of them, in their way, seemed to have led better lives than Martin Karpp, who lived out his solitary agony in a room in a small West Side walk-up and worked long hours as a short-order cook at Haskell's Hamburger Emporium on East Fortieth. Until a twitch of his finger on a trigger had brought him infamy.

Most of Karpp's identities had artistic talent. Interspersed with the notes were drawings or copies of paintings done by them. Some of the artwork seemed normal enough, even reassuringly unimaginative. Some of it conveyed a sense of madness, of fierce loneliness that pulled at the heart.

The light outside had failed. Andrews didn't remember switching on the shaded desk lamp, but he had done so unconsciously as he read Dana's notes. The windowpane across the room gave back a two-dimensional image of a man hunched over a desk, absorbed in the disarray of papers spread before him. For an instant Andrews felt a disturbing sense of unfamiliarity with the man in the windowpane.

Andrews watched the man raise his left arm and turn his wrist. Then he looked away from the window at his watch. Nine twenty-five. He was tired. His back ached. He was hungry.

Arranging the notes Dana had printed on yellow legal-size paper into a reasonably neat stack, Andrews wrapped a thick rubber band around them, folded them once and attempted to tuck them into his sport coat pocket. They wouldn't fit. He spotted a brown vinyl portfolio near the typewriter on the table, unfolded the notes and slid them inside.

With the portfolio tucked beneath his arm, he switched off the desk lamp, maneuvered his way through the darkened apartment and out into the hall.

It was easy enough to get a cab at that time of night. Andrews climbed in and gave the driver the address of his hotel. What was called for now, Andrews decided, as the cab nosed pugnaciously out into traffic, was a thick steak at the hotel restaurant, a long, relaxing shower and some deep sleep. The cab edged forward like an eager predator, seemed to sense an opening in the traffic and sprang to fill the gap. Andrews' shoulder blades pressed into the worn, firm upholstery of the rear seat.

He hadn't any suspicion that he'd been watched.

10

The Dionysus Club was exclusive and expensive. For the price, it guaranteed absolute privacy for any number of activities. Millikin had been bringing Ellen Andrews here for over a year.

On the bed in the mirrored room, she lay sprawled limply on her back beside him, one leg crooked to the side so that it lay across both of his. Millikin's eyes dispassionately surveyed her nude form, the high, firm breasts that seemed as young as she would like to be, the washboard ripple of her ribs, the long legs spoiled by knees that were unfortunately knobby. There were a few more purplish webs, like faint ink marks, just beneath the surface of the flesh on her right leg, where more tiny blood vessels had ruptured. It was something you seldom saw on a younger woman, Millikin mused in his post-coital rumination.

Ellen hadn't seemed her usual voracious self this time, he thought. She had tried, but even the various devices furnished by the management had failed to arouse her to the intensity Millikin knew she possessed. He looked up and observed them in the mirrored ceiling: two very middle-aged people, a woman kept a lean, marred version of youth by constant dieting, and a paunchy, gray-haired man whose once athletic body had taken on the consistency of pale putty despite the frequent use of sunlamps. He looked away.

64 /

"Something's bothering you," he said, to take his mind off what was bothering him.

"Nothing important," Ellen answered beside him.

He ran his fingertips over her bare, cool shoulder. "Still, something . . ."

In the quiet room, he could hear her breathing with a bellows regularity. That, too, bothered Millikin, as if it were a reminder of their mortality.

"A man came to the house to see Jerry," she said. "He told me he had an appointment, but I'm sure he didn't. I'm sure he really knew Jerry wasn't home. I can tell when men lie."

Millikin propped himself up on one reddened elbow, causing a series of slight swaying motions in the waterbed. "So what did he want?"

"He wanted to know where Jerry was. I told him New York. He asked where specifically, but I said I didn't know."

"Do you?"

"No. And I don't particularly care."

"Then?" Millikin asked.

"Then? He went away."

"Why should that disturb you?"

"He never left a name. If he really had an appointment, he'd surely have left his name."

"But you already told me you were sure he was lying about that."

"Yes, and there's something else. I remember seeing him some years ago, when Jerry was a representative, at one of those dull, formal Washington functions. He stuck in my memory because someone told me he was a spy. Just like that, they said he was a spy. I assumed with the CIA."

Now Millikin understood.

"What if they're checking on Jerry?" Ellen said. "What if they find out about us, make it all public? Jerry would almost have to divorce me then. He'd have no reason not to."

Millikin lay back on the bed and thought for a moment.

"Probably there's nothing to worry about," he said. "And even if someone did discover our arrangement, Jerry now has the clout to be able to keep it quiet."

"No one has that much clout if the media gets hold of it."

"Don't bet on it," Millikin told her. "Anyway, it wouldn't be the end of things for you if Jerry did throw you out. Worse things could happen." He reached back to a master control panel and threw a switch that brought soft music into the room.

"Worse things might," Ellen said. She rose and began to dress.

11

Andrews wasn't known in New York. And if someone did think he looked familiar, they wouldn't expect a U.S. senator to be staying at the Hayes Hotel. Still, to be on the safe side, Andrews had signed himself in as Gerald Anderson and paid in advance.

Located near the theater district, the Hayes had once been one of Manhattan's better hotels. Vestiges of elegance haunted the vast lobby, with its ornate brass bank of elevators, its inlaid marble floor that showed where the new red commercial fiber carpet didn't cover. The sweeping stairway leading to the mezzanine, where the banquet rooms were, was a tarnished work of art. Off one side of the lobby was the hotel lounge, a place of dimness, red padded leather and ancient glossy walnut, where beneath a once resplendent chandelier sat a jukebox and a Wonder Woman pinball machine. Off the opposite end of the lobby was the hotel's relatively new restaurant and coffee shop. It was clean, gave prompt service and provided simply cooked, overpriced meals.

Andrews had finished his sirloin steak. He sat now sipping coffee and gazing out the window at the passing pedestrians and cab-dominated traffic. He hadn't yet gone up to his room and still had the vinyl portfolio with him, resting on the chair next to his. He put down his coffee cup in its chipped saucer, reached over and opened the portfolio.

He withdrew the sheet of paper that most interested him—the list of people who had touched one or another of Karpp's separate personalities, not suspecting that they knew only a fragment of a man. Their names were listed neatly in a column, and after each name was their former relationship with the identity they'd known. In some cases there were addresses to go with the names.

Another sheet of paper listed each of the Karpp identities along with personality traits, habits and known activities. Andrews absently accepted a refill of coffee from a tired-looking waitress as he studied the papers before him. His heart, he was surprised to notice, was beating rapidly. For the first time he began really to understand Dana Larsen's fascination with his object of study. There were alluring shadows here where realities overlapped. There were unsettling implications.

Tomorrow Andrews would speak with some of the people who had each known one of the various pseudonymous Martin Karpps. That was something Dana Larsen probably hadn't had a chance to do before death interrupted him. Andrews glanced up and saw that the weary waitress, balancing two tall cocktails on a small red tray, was threading her way among the tables and would pass near him. Looking at her reminded him how tired he was. He signaled for the check.

The next morning Andrews awoke at a few minutes past nine and blearily looked around in temporary disorientation at the mottled green walls, thick flowered drapes and traditional plain furniture. The ceiling was high and cream colored. The paint was begining to peel. Outside in the hall a maid was pushing a linen cart with a squeaky wheel. Andrews remembered that he was at the Hayes Hotel.

He showered, toweled dry, then went down to the coffee shop. It was crowded and bright. He had a bacon omelette with toast and coffee before leaving for his first stop.

The Bayon Lounge was still in business at the same location. Feeling somewhat like a detective in a hackneyed private-eye novel, Andrews walked into the lounge, which was barren of customers, sat at the bar and asked the bartender if he knew Harry Jennings.

A fictional private eye never had it so easy. The bartender was Harry Jennings.

"Do you remember Martin Karpp?" Andrews asked.

Jennings, a large, balding man with a fogged left eye, grinned his professional warm grin. "Well, yes and no," he said. He was seated on a high stool by the cash register.

"I'm helping somebody who's doing research into his case," Andrews said. He thought about ordering a drink, but it was too early.

"You ain't government then?"

"No. Just an interested party."

"There was enough government investigators around here four years ago to scare away damn near all our business. I wouldn't want that to be starting again. I own part of the place now."

"Congratulations. But tell me about Karpp," Andrews urged.

"You mean L. C. Chambers. That's the only name I ever knew him by, until he shot Drake and got himself arrested. In here he never talked politics, only business. What the stock market was doing, rising interest rates, that sort of bullshit. And he dressed like Madison Avenue Ike, all scrubby and pin-stripe." Jennings got down off the stool and turned out to be much shorter than he'd appeared sitting. He poured two cups of coffee from the glass pot of a pour-through brewer and placed one on the bar before Andrews. "Cream? Sugar?"

Andrews said no to both and thanked him for the coffee though he'd already had two cups this morning.

"What in particular do you want to know about . . . Chambers?" Jennings asked, stirring powdered cream in his cup.

"I don't really know," Andrews said, "so tell me anything that comes to mind."

"Chambers came in here off and on for over a year, full of tall talk, running up a big bar bill. Now and then he'd pay it off in a chunk from money he got somewhere. But usually it was big talk and on the tab."

"Was he usually alone?"

"When he came in. But he came in mostly to see Leola Raymond, and often as not they left together. She was impressed by all his talk. She was nothing but surprised when it turned out he was a fry cook over on Fortieth and not Mr. Success." Jennings sipped his coffee and grimaced as if it had burned his tongue. "Maybe you want to talk to Leola."

"Definitely. Do you know where I can find her?"

"She don't come in too often anymore, but I hear she's working as a topless dancer over at the Metropole."

"Did the FBI talk to her four years ago?"

Jennings smiled and climbed back onto his stool near the register. "They talked to *everybody* within five blocks of here. They talked to the rats in the walls!"

"Has anybody else asked you about Karpp lately?"

"Nope. He's like yesterday's newspaper. Our crowd keeps current."

Andrews thanked Jennings again for the coffee and started to leave.

"Hey, mister," the bartender called, "will you ever see Karpp?"

"I might," Andrews said, his hand on the doorknob.

"Tell him Harry Jennings said hello." A white grin shot through the dimness. "I kinda liked L. C. Chambers. Everybody did."

Andrews' next stop was at a renovated brownstone on the East Side. In the airy vestibule, he saw that Norris Kelly occupied the second floor. He pressed the button by the new brass mailbox and intercom.

"Who?" an electronically nasal voice inquired.

"My name is Gerald Anderson," Andrews said. "I need to talk to Norris Kelly."

"About?"

"A matter concerning an old friend of his—Willy Bennet."

A ten count passed, then a buzzer sounded deafeningly and Andrews pushed open the door to the stairs and trudged up thick blue carpeting.

A medium-height, wiry man with a head of frizzy reddish hair was waiting for him in an open doorway at the top of the stairs. He was wearing faded, skin-tight jeans and a long-sleeved cotton shirt open to the waist to reveal several gold chains looped about his neck. "I'm Norris Kelly and step right in," he said with a puzzled smile.

The interior of Kelly's home obviously had benefited from the touch of a professional decorator. The blue carpet on the stairs extended throughout as far as Andrews could see. The walls were pale blue, the furniture expensive white French provincial. On each side of a small white brick fireplace were shelves displaying glistening crystal figurines illuminated by subtle backlighting. Cream-colored ceiling-to-floor drapes across a wide window held the harsher reality of the city at bay.

"A beautifully done room," Andrews said.

Kelly's smooth, symmetrical features expressed deep pleasure as he nodded acceptance of the compliment.

"You mentioned Willy Bennet," he said. He limped slightly as he crossed the room and motioned for Andrews to sit on a sofa upholstered in a delicate brocade. As if suddenly conscious of his limp, he sat down himself in a wing chair facing the sofa, pausing just long enough for Andrews to sit first so that decorum had been preserved.

/ 71

"Or Martin Karpp," Andrews said. "I'm helping someone do some important research on the subject of multiple personality."

Kelly crossed his legs at the knees and tilted his head. "But aren't we all multiple personalities, really?"

"Not like Martin Karpp, I'm afraid."

"Are you working with Dr. Larsen's project?" Kelly asked.

Andrews nodded.

"He was here just last week to talk with me about Willy. I was distressed to read of his death."

"He was a fine man. Everyone who knew him was distressed."

"You in particular, judging by the way you uttered that stock but heartfelt eulogy."

For some reason Andrews was irritated by Kelly's quick and accurate perception of his feelings. "Could you go over with me what Dr. Larsen asked you about Karpp?" he said.

"Well, the doctor was interested in our relationship. I told him it was a sometimes thing that started the night I brought Willy here to do some renderings."

"Renderings?"

"Drawings of my conception of how I wanted this at-the-time dreadful place to look," Kelly explained. "I decorated it myself, with Willy's assistance. He had—has—a great deal of artistic talent, you know."

"What else about Willy did you and Dr. Larsen discuss?"

"The more intimate aspects of our relationship," Kelly answered without a hint of hesitation. "There was nothing . . . unusually unusual about it. Except for now and then. Once, when I disturbed him in the predawn hours, Willy acted as if he were someone else altogether, as if I were someone else. He said some terrible things to me. I didn't understand that then. I almost do now."

"What sort of terrible things?"

"Regarding my sexual preference. Our sexual preference, actually."

"Where did you meet Willy Bennet? And how?"

"At the Clarion Bar on West Fifty-seventh. He was drinking by himself and seemed lonely. I knew why he was there, of course, why everyone was there who was drinking alone. So I joined him."

"Did anyone else in the, er—"

"Gay community?"

"Yes. Did anyone else know Willy?"

"I don't think so. But that isn't all that uncommon, society being what it is."

"What did you and Willy talk about most of the time?"

Kelly waved an arm in a graceful, encompassing arc. "This place, mainly. It didn't take long for Willy to become as enthusiastic as I about it."

"Did he ever hint that he might want to move in with you?"

"God, no! It wasn't like Willy to hint at anything. If he'd wanted to he'd have asked directly, and he never did so."

"Did you ever offer?"

"Once. Willy said no, tactfully."

"Did Dr. Larsen happen to mention to you where he'd been, whom he'd talked to besides you?"

"Sorry." Kelly shook his head no. The reddish frizz rippled like sun-touched resilient wire. "We kept to the immediate subject."

"Did he happen to say anything that struck you as odd, as if he might be in some sort of trouble?"

"Nothing whatsoever." Kelly arched an eyebrow neatly yet unaffectedly. "You don't suspect . . . ?"

Andrews shrugged. "Dr. Larsen drowned. He'd also suffered a fractured skull. That's all anyone knows."

"Of course. Well, I never thought about something like that." Kelly laced long fingers, made a steeple and raised it to the tip of his chin in contemplation. "I really wish I could recall something that might help you, but I can't."

Andrews stood up and smiled. "Thanks for trying, anyway."

Kelly rose and trailed him to the door with the slight limp. It was evident now that beneath his tight jeans one leg was considerably thinner than the other, suggesting the result of a long-ago illness.

Andrews opened the door to the stairs.

"Mr. Anderson," Kelly said wistfully beside him, "this might sound naïve, but do you think there's a chance that Willy might ever come back?"

"About as much chance as there is of Dr. Larsen coming back," Andrews said, and watched Norris Kelly nod grimly. Andrews turned away from such naked grief. He descended the plush, blue-carpeted stairs, that possibly Willy Bennet had suggested, and pulled open the heavy door to the street.

12

Dr. Laidelier had, as usual, left his office door open. As he sat at his desk, studying a stack of vouchers by the narrow beam of a bullet-shade lamp, he became aware of someone standing just inside the doorway, watching him. He ignored this insubstantial figure on the fringe of his vision and finished reading about the purchase of sides of beef for the sanitarium kitchen.

When he pinched the bridge of his nose in weariness and then looked up, he saw that his visitor was Joseph Morgan. Probably Morgan wanted to talk with him again about re-shuffling the night hours of the security force.

"It's late, Joseph," Dr. Laidelier said. In the harsh light from the lamp, his eyes were invisible, in deep shadow beneath his prodigious gray eyebrows.

"I've been doing some investigating," Morgan said. He walked farther into the office and stood with a calm hand resting lightly on a chair.

Laidelier motioned for him to sit down. "Investigating?"

"Asking some questions in town," Morgan said, choosing to remain standing. "I thought, just for possible reference, it might be a good idea to check out some of what Senator Andrews mentioned."

"The senator is still a comparatively young man, Joseph. I

got the impression that he was unduly upset with himself over the death of a friend."

"He is a U.S. senator, though. And he was a friend of Larsen."

Dr. Laidelier pushed his glasses higher up onto his nose and studied Morgan. The coolly competent security chief didn't seem to be in any sort of an agitated state. He was merely doing his job, prudently touching bases.

"Martin Karpp told me that Larsen claimed he got a threatening note at his motel," Morgan said. "Signed Paul Liggett."

Dr. Laidelier's only indication of surprise was a shifting of his long frame in his chair. This must be the evidence Andrews had mentioned.

"I talked to the desk man at the Clover Motel," Morgan said. "He remembers a message for Dr. Larsen. He says the doctor read it right there at the desk and seemed to be rattled. Larsen grilled him on who had delivered the message, but the desk man hadn't been on duty when it came. The girl who had been at the desk said she'd been busy when the message was given to her by a man to put in Larsen's box. She could only describe the man as kind of stockily built. She barely glanced at his features and doesn't remember a thing about them, not even the color of his hair."

"Did Dr. Larsen mention that Paul Liggett's name was on the note?" Dr. Laidelier asked.

Morgan did sit down now as he shook his head. "No. The motel people are certain that he didn't mention who it was from. Maybe somebody was joking with Larsen. Or maybe Larsen was joking with Senator Andrews. But we can be certain of one thing: whoever's signature was on it, there was a note."

"Very well," Dr. Laidelier agreed patiently, "there was a note."

"Then I went to the Chicken Barn," Morgan went on.

"Chicken coop, you mean?"

"Barn," Morgan said. "It's a restaurant right outside of town. They told me at the motel that Dr. Larsen always ate supper there. I asked all the employees if they could remember anything unusual about Dr. Larsen. I found out that a waitress had told Larsen about a man coming into the restaurant looking for him, and Larsen seemed to get upset, especially when the waitress described the man."

"And whose description was it?" Dr. Laidelier asked, anticipating the answer.

"I don't know," Morgan said.

"Didn't you ask the waitress?"

"No, I got all this secondhand. The waitress is dead."

"Ah," Dr. Laidelier said, as if at last his keenest interest had been aroused. "Dead how?"

"She fell down the cellar stairs in her house," Morgan said. "Broken neck."

Both men sat quietly for a while, not looking at one another. Morgan began to drum on the arm of his chair with the knuckle of his right forefinger, the same monotonous tapping, over and over.

Finally Dr. Laidelier asked, "Did you discover anything else?"

"No," Morgan said, stopping the tapping, "that's all."

"Any conclusions?"

"Not firm ones. I just thought you should know about what these people told me."

"It could pertain," Dr. Laidelier said. "You don't think Martin Karpp, or some part of Martin Karpp, is leaving the sanitarium and terrorizing the countryside, do you?"

"Of course not," Morgan said. "That's the one thing that can be ruled out. As far as I'm concerned, the matter's closed. It closed with Dr. Larsen's death. I was only satisfying curiosity and tying loose ends."

"Which is as it should be," Dr. Laidelier said.

Morgan stood up and walked to the door. "At least we know that Senator Andrews is on the level, not inventing a reason to scrutinize us."

"I never suspected that," Dr. Laidelier said, and he hadn't.

"I did, I'll admit," Morgan said. "I guess I'm too much of a skeptic."

"That's your job," Dr. Laidelier reassured him.

Morgan smiled. "It is at that. Good night, Doctor."

After Morgan had left, Dr. Laidelier switched off the lamp and walked from his office. He strode down a corridor, opened a door with a large key from the ring on his belt and began making his way across the narrow stretch of grass to his bungalow that was located on the sanitarium grounds behind the main building.

There was no sound other than the doctor's rustling footsteps in the black grass, no normal background trill of crickets. Pesticides had eliminated most of the insects on the grounds. It was best that way. The inmates were extraordinarily inventive with insects.

Inside his bungalow, Dr. Laidelier relaxed with his nightly glass of port before bed and thought about what Joseph Morgan had told him. There were, the doctor decided, a good many rational explanations for what Morgan had found out. A practical joke. Then someone happening to resemble Martin Karpp—at least to the waitress—when he asked for Dr. Larsen in the restaurant. Or perhaps Larsen had wanted to perpetrate a joke and laid the groundwork for it. Or maybe Larsen had been setting himself up for a lucrative book of some sort to be marketed to the occult-hungry public. Larsen hadn't seemed like such a man, but who could tell? And the waitress's death? An accident. The simplest, and therefore probably correct, answer.

Dr. Laidelier savored the last sweet sip of port and decided to go to bed. Without thinking about it, he crossed the room and locked the front door.

A step away from the door, he stood still and smiled. Usually he left the door unlocked. At this time of night, all the patients were in their quarters, behind brick walls, and no one other than Security was on the grounds.

Dr. Laidelier thought about unlocking the door, if only to prove something to himself. Then he decided that was reactive and unnecessary. Whether the door was locked or unlocked was unimportant, after all.

As he ambled into his bedroom he was chuckling, chiding himself. He had studied in Berlin under Steinmetz. Dr. Steinmetz, though quite cognizant of the power of mind over body, did not believe that a man could walk through solid walls.

And neither did any of his disciples believe that.

13

Music blared from the open doorway of the Metropole, spilling out over the sun-warmed street to lose itself in the din of Times Square. A huge bearded black man stood outside the doorway, glibly trying to entice passersby inside. A large percentage of the people on the crowded sidewalk were tourists, some of whom paused and gawked in through the door at the two topless dancers gyrating almost mechanically on the lighted bartop stage, but the fast-talking, cajoling barker was having no luck in attempting to get someone actually to walk inside and spend money for a drink.

"Topless!" the bearded man yelled at Andrews, as if he himself couldn't quite believe it. "Step on in an' check 'em out!"

Andrews, the waist-length jacket he had bought unbuttoned over his black turtleneck sweater, stood for a moment beneath the lighted marquee that was blinking futilely against the bright daylight. He could see the shimmering, spotlighted flesh of one of the dancers as she strutted back and forth on the bar, her lean body jerking almost casually in rhythm with the repetitious, high-decibel drumbeat. Her ribs showed, and her frantically jiggling bare breasts were small; it occurred to Andrews that such constant dancing would melt away every inch of excess weight from a woman.

"Check it out up close, brother!" the bearded man invited through a jovial, lascivious grin. He appeared slightly surprised when Andrews walked past him and inside.

As Andrews slid into one of the booths along the wall, his eyes became accustomed to the dimness and he saw that there were only three other customers, one of whom had his head resting on the bar, his eyes closed, his mind oblivious to the spiked high heels that cavorted sometimes inches from his tousled hair and empty glass. One of the dancers, the lean brunette he'd seen from the sidewalk, caught Andrews' eye and smiled as she went into a series of bumps to keep up with the gradually increasing mad tempo of the drums. Andrews smiled back. He couldn't help but think of the many Washington columnists who would love to see him now. How the media could distort. How they could separate the public man from the private.

A waitress appeared alongside the booth, and Andrews ordered a scotch and seltzer. He watched the brunette and her tiny blond partner dance out of sync as the music's tempo became even more driving and demanding. He wondered if the brunette was Leola Raymond.

She wasn't. When the waitress arrived with Andrews' drink, she told him in answer to his question that Leola Raymond was the tiny blonde, and that she was due to take a break at the end of this number.

Andrews turned his attention to Leola Raymond, who was graceful but not highly trained as a dancer. She had a massive mop of wavy blond hair that flounced about as she danced, making her delicate features appear almost absurdly doll-like.

"Will you tell her I'd like to talk with her when she's finished?" Andrews asked the waitress.

She withdrew one of the swizzle sticks that were laced in the wide network of her black stockings and set it down daintily on the napkin next to Andrews' drink. "The girls here don't fraternize," she said.

"I don't want to fraternize any further than talking to her about a mutual friend, L. C. Chambers. Will you tell her that?" He slipped a five-dollar bill into the waitress's hand, which was amazingly convenient. "Tell her my name is Anderson."

The waitress barely glanced at him. "I'll tell her, Mr. Anderson."

Andrews' glass was empty by the time the drums ceased their relentless beat and the dancers left the stage. He hoped that Leola Raymond would have enough breath left to talk if she did agree to see him. He ordered another drink and asked the waitress to bring one of whatever Leola usually liked.

"She ain't allowed," the waitress said. "But I told her what you asked."

Andrews nodded and waited.

Ten minutes later Leola Raymond walked fully dressed to his booth. Though she still wore her high-heeled shoes, she appeared shorter than she had onstage, maybe only about five feet tall. The lithe hips that had gyrated so rapidly were now covered by a black skirt of some kind of velvety material, and beneath a white long-sleeved blouse was not the slightest hint of breasts. She might have been twelve years old but for the unnerving directness of her blue eyes and the controlled stiffness of her delicate face. Andrews stood without speaking, and she nodded and sat down, as if it had all been choreographed.

He lowered himself back into the booth. "They told me you couldn't drink on the job," he said.

She nodded again. It was a triumph over gravity that her piled blond hair stayed in place; it appeared soft, unmolded by hair spray. "I don't drink anyway."

"Harry Jennings, over at the Bayon Lounge, suggested I talk to you," Andrews told her. "He said you might know some things about Martin Karpp. Or L. C. Chambers, as you knew him."

In the dim light her smile seemed to jump across the table. "Chambers I knew, but I didn't know Martin Karpp. And my Chambers wouldn't have shot somebody—not for any political reason."

"When he was arrested, is that the first you heard of Karpp?"

"It sure was. Far as I knew, L. C. Chambers was exactly what he seemed, a big, happy kinda guy that had made his pile and liked good times. I liked good times too, so we got together and had 'em."

"Why 'liked'?"

The child's body squirmed beneath the blouse and skirt. Andrews noticed now the protrusion of her nipples beneath the thin white material, rising and falling with her breathing or her heartbeat.

"I got more serious about L.C. than I let on," she said, "even to him. When it happened—when he shot Drake and got arrested and it came out—it was like the world turned around and kicked me in the box again, only this time harder than ever, so as to show me things would never change, only look like they were gonna. After that and a few other things happened, times didn't seem so good anymore no matter what I did."

Andrews found himself trying to guess her age in the faint light. Without being too obvious he looked at her neck, the backs of her hands, the traces of makeup-smoothed facial lines. Thirty at least, he decided. And she must have gotten there in a hurry. He was curious. "Where are you from?" he asked. "You don't have a New York accent."

"Chicago. The windy city." A smile. "Maybe that's why I liked L.C."

"He talked a lot?"

"About everything. About what he owned, what he was gonna buy." A laugh broke from her. "And he was a goddamn cook in a ptomaine house a couple of blocks from here!" She studied her thin hands, pale against the dark table. "Hell, if he'd told me, I was to the point I wouldn't have much cared."

"It wasn't the way you might think," Andrews said, suddenly feeling sorry for her. "He wasn't pretending to be somebody else in order to impress you; he *was* somebody else. And more than one person. The doctors *do* know that; his case isn't the only one of its kind."

"I know. Since L.C., I read about others. That woman who was all those people, most of the time not even remembering. She had a shitty childhood like me."

"So did Martin Karpp."

The music began again, the monotonous, driving drumbeat. The brunette was dancing again on the bar-level stage, elbows back, breasts thrust forward, eyes straight ahead and gazing at nothing. The drunk at the bar had come around and was staring up at her as if confused by her presence but reluctant to leave.

"Did Dr. Larsen talk to you?" Andrews asked Leola. It was difficult to be understood through the music. She cupped a hand to her ear and he repeated the question.

She shook her head no and mouthed, "I have to get back now."

"Can I talk to you again?" Andrews asked, almost shouting.

She hesitated, then plucked a ball-point pen from his shirt pocket and scribbled a phone number on the napkin beneath his drink. As she stood to leave, she took the pen again and wrote beneath the number "Mostly during the days." She walked away without smiling, dark skirt swaying as if blown by the music.

Andrews sat and finished his drink. A man and a woman stepped through the door, saw the topless dancer, exchanged glances and went back out into the shadowless glare of daylight. They looked like solid, upstanding citizens, Andrews thought. Voters. He wondered if he was out of his mind doing what he'd been doing the past several days. Maybe he was developing another personality himself. There were moments lately when he didn't at all see himself as a U.S. senator. The blood in his veins flowed too fast and too hot for grave deliberation and reasoned debate, for the pragmatic subtleties of the office. Maybe he should get back to the perceptible realities of his life, phone Judy Carnegie and let her know how to reach him in case anything urgent occurred. He needed a connecting thread. A touchstone.

But she would wonder what he was doing at a place like the Hayes. What he was doing in that area of Manhattan. She would worry. She wouldn't understand or approve of what he was doing because of Dana Larsen's death. Judy Carnegie: a cool mind and a fervent player of the game. Andrews rattled the ice in his empty glass. Maybe she should be the senator.

Leola Raymond was onstage again, dancing with the same amicable, bored expression as her partner's. Andrews looked at her pampered, almost translucent flesh and thought of Pat Colombo. Then, despite himself, he thought of Ellen. Ellen was built somewhat like Leola. That thin, only taller and without the impression of child-woman fragility.

Leola's mascara-widened blue eyes rotated in their sockets like the mechanical eyes of a mannequin, and deadpan she returned Andrews' stare. He nodded to her, then got up and made his way out, accompanied by the eerie knowledge that he was walking stride for stride in the footsteps of Martin Karpp.

14

Harry Jennings took a few moments of his free time away from mixing drinks to wipe down the bar hastily near the table-order serving area. The Bayon Lounge was crowded, as it usually was on Friday nights, with a combination of out-of-towners and the local regulars. Plenty of talk, plenty of laughter and plenty of drinking. Jennings liked it that way. If the Bayon thrived, he figured to get an automatic raise soon through the deal he had with majority owner Jack Mannering.

Sonya, the barmaid, glided up, adjusted her almost non-existent skirt and yelled "Piña colada!"

Jesus, Jennings thought, that must be the fiftieth piña colada of the evening. He turned to the backbar, reached for the Bacardi and set about building the drink. He hoped the same customer hadn't ordered all fifty.

Jennings had the drink mixed in less than a minute, handed it over to Sonya and rang up the sale. Something—he wasn't sure what—made him think about L. C. Chambers as he worked behind the bar. He wondered if the guy who had been in the other day, Anders or Anderson, had found out what he needed to know.

What could you say about Chambers? Who would suspect a friendly, self-important and smooth Mr. Success like L.C. could turn out to be a Martin Karpp, political assassin? Of course, to believe the headshrinkers and this guy Anderson,

L.C. *was* L.C., at least when he was being L.C. Confusing.

Through the grayish haze of tobacco smoke, Jennings saw the short, thickset figure of Jack Mannering approaching the bar. Mannering was dressed sharply as usual, wearing a dark suit and flashing his gold cufflinks. Ever since the price of gold had skyrocketed, Mannering had taken to wearing tons of the stuff. As he rested his elbow on the bar, his sleeve rode up to reveal a gold wristwatch. He wore a gold pinky ring on each hand as well as his customary diamond on his left ring finger.

"Profitable night, heh?" he said, smiling his crooked, yellowish smile. Almost a gold smile.

"Busy as hell," Jennings said. "You'd think the drinks were free."

Mannering's smile lost candlepower. "Just so they ain't." No doubt who owned the biggest piece of the place. He fired up a long cigar to add to the almost solid haze of smoke. "Did a guy come around to talk to you about Martin Karpp?" he asked.

Jennings nodded. "A few days ago. Anderson was his name."

"Anderson wasn't the name of the guy who came in here and asked me a lot of questions," Mannering said. "Come to think of it, he never left a name. At least not one I can recall."

"There was a doctor, a psychiatrist, that came around before Anderson," Jennings said. He interrupted the conversation to put together two scotch and waters. When he returned, he said, "He was doing research of some kind on whatever ailed L. C. Chambers."

"My man never mentioned being a doctor," Mannering said. "But it don't matter. What matters is I want you to be uncooperative if anybody else comes in prying about L. C. Chambers or Karpp or whoever or whatever he is."

Jennings frowned as Sonya placed an order slip on the bar. "How uncooperative?"

Mannering looked at him and shrugged. "Just don't remember anything. That ain't a crime. Four years ago, when Drake was shot and killed, it wasn't a week before everybody from the press to the CIA started coming in here asking questions. The trouble is, none of them bought drinks. The whole deal wasn't good for business. It brought in a few touristy types, but it scared away a lot of the regulars. And all these official job-doers can be a pain in the ass."

"That I remember," Jennings said. He handed Sonya's scrawled order slip to the part-time bartender, who was looking desperate about falling behind in his work.

"Don't make a big deal out of it," Mannering said. "You know what I mean? Just play dumb."

"No problem there, boss,"

Mannering looked at Jennings and winked, grinning as he stood away from the bar. "I've always known better, Harry."

"Regular?" Jennings asked, inquiring whether Mannering wanted his usual Smirnoff's on the rocks with a twist of lime, ignoring the compliment.

"Not tonight, Harry." Mannering lifted a gold-adorned hand in a parting wave, turned and disappeared into the haze and milling mass of customers.

Probably going out to get some breathable air, Jennings thought, and wished he could do the same. Instead, he turned to the backbar to help catch up with the drink orders. He understood what Mannering meant about the official nosy Petes who might come in snooping about Karpp all over again. But he didn't see why he had to be uncooperative with everyone else who might ask about the matter. Still, if Mannering wanted him to be dumb, dumb he would be and then some. He was smart enough to do that.

Jennings was setting three martinis on the serving bar when for some reason a man's voice seemed to disengage itself from the steady buzz of lounge chatter, as occasionally a voice will do in a crowded place. "Sorry," the voice said, "my mistake," as if its owner might be apologizing for stepping on someone's toe.

Idly Jennings glanced in the general direction of the voice. He almost dropped the glass he was holding as he glimpsed a squarish, broad-shouldered figure squeezing through the crowd and heading for the door.

Jennings swallowed. "Chambers!" he murmured, without realizing he'd spoken.

But it couldn't be. Jennings blinked. The figure was gone.

Had the voice that attracted Jennings' attention been Chambers'? What precisely had it said? He tried to recall the voice exactly and couldn't pin it in his memory. For that matter, he couldn't exactly recall the voice of L. C. Chambers. It had, after all, been four years since he'd heard it.

But there was an uncanny familiarity about the figure he'd glimpsed. It was almost as if his thoughts had summoned it from the past. The grayish tobacco smoke in the lounge seemed suddenly to become a frosty, chilling fog. Maybe something like that actually had happened. Why not? There were creepy things happening in this world every day, so why not to him?

Sonya crossed his line of vision, waving a fistful of orders and rolling her eyes. He was aware of her placing the orders on the bar, hurrying away with a tray of mixed drinks.

Jennings realized he was standing motionless. Time to get busy. Customers were waiting. He told himself that he was imagining things because of his conversation with Mannering. Imagination could be a sonofabitch.

Shaking his head, he neatly flipped a jigger of bourbon into the glass he was holding and concentrated on his work, his work and nothing else. Ice, liquor, soda, twist of lime or lemon. He let the part-time man handle the beer.

Within a hectic half hour he forgot about L. C. Chambers. Almost.

15

Where were the last few days taking him? Andrews wondered as he hailed a cab in front of the New York Public Library and gave the driver the address of Bargain Electronics. Like almost everything else that formed the basis of his recent movements, he'd gotten the address from Dana Larsen's notes.

Andrews had spent the last six hours at the library, poring over what scant material he could find on multiple personality. He had absorbed everything available on the subject, from Mendell's *Theories on Fragmented Personalities* to the popular literature *Three Faces of Eve* and *Sybil*. The phenomenon was still relatively new to psychiatry, not nearly so well understood as most of the more common mental abberations.

What Andrews had gotten the most of for his effort was eyestrain. Not to mention an aching back from studiously bending over a library table. He consoled himself with the idea that some bit of information he'd picked up that now seemed irrelevant could in the future become important if not pivotal. That was often how thorough research on any subject paid dividends.

But he had to admit that his hours of study had left him more disoriented than enlightened. And for some reason he kept thinking about Dana Larsen and the extraordinarily high suicide rate among psychiatrists.

The taxi turned several corners and was neatly threading

its way through jammed and angry traffic. Horns blasted occasional tuneless fierce music that was met with indifference. Andrews sat in the back of the cab and watched the throngs of pedestrians.

Outside the cab, the elegantly dressed strolled blindly past blind beggars in front of exclusive shops. Tourists with 35-millimeter cameras ignored a drunk leaning in a doorway as they walked with eyes raised, looking for a good shot for future slide shows at home. Andrews had been to Manhattan many times, but never before had he noticed the vivid contrasts, the shades of unreality. It was as if he were just beginning to discover the dark side of some moon.

"Which side of the street?" the cabbie asked, interrupting Andrews' disconcerting reverie.

"Over there on the right, by the place with the sign that looks like a radio."

Andrews paid the cabbie and got out onto the sidewalk. He stood looking at Bargain Electronics. Two angled show windows led like the gleaming walls of a funnel back to an open door. Behind the windows were glittering displays of radios, tape players, TVs, video recorders, cameras and accessories, calculators, typewriters, apparently anything that plugged into an electrical outlet or was powered by batteries. Andrews walked between the banks of dials, aerials, lenses, knobs and glistening plastic, into the similarly cluttered interior of the overstocked shop.

A few customers were poking about a merchandise table in the rear, and a swarthy young man was seated behind a counter watching them with something like contempt.

"Are you Vincent Grammo?" Andrews asked him.

The youth didn't bother looking at Andrews. "In the back," he said. "You want him?"

"I need to talk with him."

The man still hadn't budged, still stared at the shop's clientele with venomous dark eyes. "Sellin'?" he asked Andrews.

"No, I just want to talk with Grammo. Tell him I'm here. My name's Anderson."

But apparently the counterman had pressed a button that sounded a buzzer somewhere in the rear of the shop. A short, potbellied man in his late fifties, with graying hair and classic Latin features tugged at by age, stepped from a doorway that had been concealed in the paneling. He looked about curiously.

"Wants to talk to you," the youth behind the counter said, jerking a thumb in Andrews' direction in a gesture somehow disdainful.

Andrews stepped over to Grammo and offered his hand. "About Alan Hobson," he said. Grammo shook the hand and exerted a slight pressure in the direction of the other end of the long counter, where they could talk privately. Both men walked as far as possible while still being separated by the counter and stopped near a bright yellow display of Kodak film.

"You FBI?" Grammo asked. He braced his elbows on the counter. He was the perfect height for that.

"No," Andrews said, "I'm helping to do some research into Martin Karpp."

"You mean Hobson. That's who he was to me, so that's how I think of the poor bastard. Did you know Dr. Larsen?"

"Very well," Andrews said.

"He was in here about a week ago, asking about Hobson. Next thing you know I pick up the paper and he's dead. Drowned."

"I know," Andrews said. "What did Dr. Larsen ask you about? So we aren't covering the same ground."

"Just generally about Hobson. Nothing specific I can recall. He was supposed to come back so we could talk again. Said he might work his information into a book. Christ, you can make a million dollars that way nowadays, providing you can't write."

"When did you realize Hobson had been stealing from you?" Andrews asked.

Grammo shook his head and exposed Hollywood-perfect teeth in a grin. "Never. Not until it came out he was Martin Karpp, and when they searched his apartment after the shooting and discovered all the stock from here. That's when I found out. He had a method of doctoring the invoices. Mind you, I'd have caught on to it eventually. Would have had to. But he got away with over three thousand dollars' worth retail in the six months he worked here."

Andrews understood now where "L. C. Chambers" had gotten his good-time money.

"Them other guys he talked about, I figured they was real," Grammo remarked ruefully. "You never do really know anybody, I guess, maybe not even yourself."

"Other guys?"

"Sure. Chambers, Liggett. And the queer, Bennet."

"What about Jay Jefferson?"

"That's who Karpp claimed he was when he killed Drake, ain't it?"

Andrews nodded.

Grammo rubbed his square chin. "Yeah, I think he mentioned that name too. Hell, seems to me he even mentioned Martin Karpp, but I ain't sure. He didn't talk about these 'people' a lot, you know. But when he did, it was as if they was casual acquaintances."

"Did Dr. Larsen mention anyone else he'd talked to? Anyone he planned to talk to, or where he was going?"

"No, we just talked for a while about Hobson."

Andrews continued to probe, attempting to find out what Dana Larsen had discovered or tried to discover, searching for some link with death by drowning in the Hudson River. "Tell me more about Alan Hobson," he said.

Grammo was eager to talk about his now infamous ex-clerk. "He only worked here part time, in the evenings. He said he had some other job, but to tell you the truth I forget where. It wasn't his real job as a cook, though. I'd have remembered that." Grammo shrugged. "Hell, you'd have figured him for normal. A nice kid, actually. Didn't know a lot about electronics, but I figured he was eager—and, yeah, honest. Clean-cut, they used to call kids like that." Grammo straightened his stocky body and squinted his bullfighter's eyes. "I don't know what surprised me most, that he was Karpp or Jefferson or whoever the hell and had shot Drake, or that he'd been stealing from me. I mean, the stealing was more personal."

"But you don't sound as if you hold a grudge."

"Hell, the man was sick. I got a sister been committed since she was twelve. Head injury from an accident. I understand."

Four young Puerto Ricans entered the shop, suddenly filling it with movement and noise. One of them had a portable tape player slung over his bony shoulder by a wide colorful strap. The deep throb of a bass and the wail of a clarinet blared from the oversized speaker. They began to browse, moving to the beat of the music, fingering merchandise nervously.

"Anything else?" Grammo asked Andrews.

Andrews said there wasn't.

Grammo yelled, "Shut that damn thing off, hey?" as he moved down the counter toward the four boys. They ignored his request and exchanged a few probably disdainful remarks in Spanish.

"You got any leftover cassettes?" one of the boys asked.

"Get fucked," replied the swarthy youth behind the counter.

As Andrews walked from the shop, Vincent Grammo was trying to make peace and sell a tape cassette. The music was still blaring at top volume, maybe even louder than before. Buyer enjoyed a certain advantage over seller.

When he returned to his hotel room, Andrews saw immediately that the brown vinyl portfolio containing Dana Larsen's notes was gone from where he'd left it on the desk. He cursed himself aloud, unmercifully and artfully, for not being more careful.

But no one was supposed to know he was here. No one!

His heart seemed to double-pump as it responded to a jolt of adrenaline. Quickly he went to the door and threw the bolt to lock it even against a hotel pass key.

The telephone rang.

Andrews let it jangle three times before snatching up the receiver and pressing it to his ear hard enough to cause pain. "Hello!" The mocking click and buzz of a severed connection was his only answer.

He replaced the receiver slowly, as if handling explosives. Why would anyone call him and then hang up? To make sure he was in his room?

Of course it might have been the hotel management, a mistake, a switchboard plug in the wrong socket, a visitor in the lobby who'd used a house phone and dialed the wrong room and hung up. There were a lot of innocent explanations for the phone call. Andrews couldn't accept any of them.

He grabbed his sport coat and left the room. The hall was empty. He walked toward the elevators, then past them to a corner near a window and an obviously artificial plant whose pot had been used frequently for a trash receptacle. He stood partly concealed and watched the elevators. If anyone did get out on this floor and walk to the door to his room, Andrews would be able to get into the elevator and descend before whoever it might be would have a chance to react and run down nearly the entire length of the hall to try to stop him.

Five minutes passed, not easily.

Then Andrews heard the thumping and grinding of the old elevator rising toward the twentieth floor. He licked his lips and waited, hoping the elevator would ascend past him to one of the floors above.

It stopped.

Cables thrummed softly within the shaft as the elevator adjusted to be level with the hall floor, and the sliding doors opened with a ratchety hiss.

Andrews pressed himself back out of sight until he heard the elevator doors close. Then he peered around the corner and saw that a woman was walking along the hall toward his door. She was a tall woman, wearing a stylish green dress and carrying a large paper bag of the sort department stores give customers. The bag crackled briskly with each of her steps.

She didn't stop at Andrews' door. Instead she walked all the way to the end of the hall, took a key from her purse, opened another door and disappeared inside her own room.

The hall was quiet again.

Andrews realized that his jaw was aching from the pressure of clenching his teeth. He told himself to relax. If anyone was coming up after him they would have been here by now. But to be on the safe side, he'd wait another ten minutes.

As time slowly edged the hands of his watch, Andrews heard elevators pass the twentieth floor several times. But none again stopped to deliver a passenger.

Andrews decided it would be safe to return to his room now, but he didn't feel like going there. Instead he took an elevator down to the lobby and went out for a walk.

It was much cooler outside, and the side of the street he walked was deeply shadowed. With only his sport coat for extra warmth, he was uncomfortable. He kept to the curb side of the pavement, staying in the midst of the flow of pedestrians going in his direction. Around him voices were discussing jobs and romances and petty despairs. Snatches of private lives. Andrews felt again that almost panicky sense of detachment he'd experienced earlier that day.

He forced calm on himself and considered his options. It would be pointless to change hotels. Whoever was watching him would simply pick up his trail again when he continued to dig into Dana Larsen's activities the week before Dana's death, then follow him to his new hotel.

The thing to do was to stay where he was but make sure that he was secure. Check the room whenever he entered, get a good secondary lock, a traveler's lock, for the door. And when he was out he'd leave a paper match stuck between door and frame, so that if anyone entered it would drop onto the hall carpet. He'd seen that done several times in movies and on TV. The thought of giving up and returning to Washington occurred to Andrews but was quickly rejected. His fear and his determination were increasing in direct proportion to each other. This current was not too swift for him; he would swim farther.

He knew that his present attitude had literally gotten him into deep water before. Every strong swimmer who ever drowned stroked under that same misconception. Perhaps even Dana Larsen.

It was time to seek advice, Andrews decided, as well as reassurance.

When he got back to his room, he would phone Pat Colombo for both.

16

The one thing that Leola Raymond feared more than anything else was cancer. Her mother had died from cancer of the uterus after refusing for years to accept medical treatment. Hesitancy born of fear had cost her the price of a painful death at forty-five years of age.

Leola remembered her mother's face when she had come home from seeing the doctor she'd finally gone to for a firm diagnosis. And Leola could still feel the quiet terror of those long visits in the County Hospital cancer ward.

So regardless of whatever happened in her life, or what her financial position was at the moment, every six months Leola went to Dr. Anthony Tonella for a pap test. Tonella understood and always phoned her as soon as the laboratory report on her smear was in. Leola suffered while waiting for those phone calls.

Dr. Tonella had his office in a run-down building on West Forty-second Street. The office was small, the waiting room dusty and disarranged. Tonella's reputation as a physician wasn't the best, and there were rumors that he supplied certain prescription drugs illegally to his acquaintances. But Leola knew that in the late mornings, after probable hangovers and before a high level of his day's alcoholic ration, Dr. Tonella was as skilled as a high-priced Park Avenue society doctor. And more compassionate.

Leola glanced at her watch and saw that it was five minutes to eleven. She always arrived early for her appointments. She was alone in the waiting room. Dr. Tonella had no receptionist, and Leola had rung the bell when she'd entered. She had heard Dr. Tonella call something to her from the inner office, and she sat down to wait.

Tonella wasn't the sort of doctor to lavish money on magazine subscriptions, so the small waiting room was supplied with stacks of old newspapers. Nervously, Leola picked up a six-month-old *Post* and began leafing through it. She read the gossip and advice columns and then put the paper on the bottom of the stack and picked up the top paper, which was only slightly more recent.

As she was searching for Ann Landers' column, a photograph on page five caught her attention. She sat still, then awkwardly and noisily folded the paper into tight quarters, as if a firm bulkiness behind the grainy black-and-white photo would lend it more dimension and clarity.

The photograph was of three U.S. senators descending the steps of the Capitol Building in Washington, D.C. The caption beneath the photo described them as possible proponents of something called the water appropriations bill. One of the men in the photograph was Gerald Anderson, only in the paper he was identified as Jerry Andrews—Senator Jerry Andrews.

Leola stared intently at the photograph, her neck craned forward. She felt a stirring of anger at being deceived, then confusion. Anderson, or Andrews, hadn't acted like a U.S. senator. Then Leola realized that she had never before met a senator of any sort and had no basis for comparison.

But Andrews was young, with a kind of male attractiveness not usually associated with dry bureaucracy. And if he really was such a big shot, why was he hanging around the Metropole asking questions about L. C. Chambers? Surely the CIA or

FBI didn't send around somebody like that to pry.

Leola's confusion jelled into resolve. Anderson-Andrews owed her some answers.

The door to the inner office opened with a subdued squeak, and Dr. Tonella took a step into the reception room and smiled at Leola. She saw instantly that he appeared sober, and his fingernails were clean.

"You're next, Miss Raymond," he said with professional smoothness, as if the waiting room were crowded.

Leola nodded and smiled back. "Do you mind if I tear something out of your newspaper?" she asked.

Dr. Tonella shrugged bunchy shoulders beneath his not-so-clean white coat. "Go ahead," he told Leola. "I won't charge you for it."

He waited patiently while she carefully folded the paper and tore out the photograph of the three very dignified figures on the Capitol steps.

Andrews experienced an unexpected elation when Leola Raymond phoned him at his hotel. She said she wanted to talk to him about the L. C. Chambers matter, and she suggested that they meet at the Howard Johnson's Restaurant near Times Square.

Andrews arrived ten minutes early for their appointment, but as he entered the restaurant he saw Leola sitting alone at a table near the booths that lined a long wall. He informed the smiling hostess that he was meeting someone, walked to Leola's table and sat down. She looked at him gravely over the rim of a glass containing what appeared to be chocolate milkshake. Her pale cheeks collapsed inward as she sucked on the straw.

"Are you always early?" she asked, setting down the glass. A fleck of the thick liquid clung to a corner of her mouth.

"Punctual, anyway," Andrews said, grinning at her. He got the impression that she was a little rattled and embarrassed over being caught drinking a milkshake. "That stuff will destroy your figure," he said.

"You talk like my boss."

"That's why he is the boss."

"No, he's the boss and I'm the dancer because I've got no education and he's got no tits."

Andrews laughed. "I guess that's an accurate assessment at that." A waitress brought him a glass of water and a menu. Just for the hell of it, he ordered a chocolate milkshake.

"You should have ordered an egg in it," Leola said, after the waitress had left. "You're on an expense account, aren't you, Senator?"

Andrews felt the impact of surprise in the pit of his stomach. His face gave no hint of what was going on below. An occupational habit of duplicity, useless at this point. "How did you find out?" he asked.

"I saw your picture in an old newspaper." Leola took another hard-earned sip of the thick milkshake while she regarded him. "Why did you lie?" she asked.

"Because if my identity were known, it would attract a certain amount of publicity. That would make it difficult for me to make inquiries, and it would create problems for me and for the people I ask about Martin Karpp."

"But why are you asking questions about Karpp? He's been declared insane, and he's in a sanitarium for life."

Andrews appraised the woman across the table from him, the ridiculous blond hairdo, the supple dancer's body gracing slacks and a soft gray sweater. There was no guile in her, he decided. Not because she was stupid, but because she simply was honest. It shone through her eyes and was reflected in her attractive, fine-boned features. The politician in him sensed a quid pro quo. He decided to be honest with her; she had been, and would continue to be, honest with him. And he was sure she would keep his identity a secret.

While Leola sat finishing her milkshake, and Andrews' own

sat untouched, he told her everything, beginning with Dana Larsen's visit in Washington.

When he was finished, he saw Leola shiver. "It's . . . weird," she said, after a futile search for words. "I could never imagine L.C. actually killing anyone or anything. I don't suppose I ever believed down deep that he and Martin Karpp were really the same man."

"There isn't any doubt that they're not, in a sense. And yet they are. Even Martin Karpp realizes that, in his own way."

"And now you need for me to keep quiet," Leola said.

For an instant Andrews thought she might intend to extort money from him in exchange for her silence, and he actually considered paying her. In the next instant, he was ashamed of his suspicion.

"For me to be quiet," Leola told him, "I need to be able to trust you."

"And do you trust me?"

"Yes."

Andrews was somewhat surprised by the abruptness of her answer. "Why?" he asked.

Leola gave a little toss of her complexly coiffed head. "Intuition, I guess. Because of your eyes."

"The windows to the soul and all that?"

Leola didn't smile. "Maybe they really are. Anyway, I won't say anything about who you are, Senator Andrews."

"It's Jerry Andrews. Just Jerry to you, Leola."

"Sure, Mr. Future President."

They both laughed. Andrews was deeply touched by her ingenuousness. There was nothing devious about their arrangement. She simply liked him, and so she trusted him until he might give her reason to think otherwise. Hers was a painful but logical philosophy she had no doubt paid for dearly but would never change. Andrews admired her. He admired her a lot.

"Have you had dinner?" he asked.

"This milkshake was my dinner. I've gotta get to work for the early evening show." She stood up, and he stood also.

Andrews touched her shoulder with the tips of his fingers, feeling a warm energy radiate to him from beneath the sweater. "I appreciate this, Leola. I won't forget it."

Her smile was genuine, not the one instinctively engineered for those who watched her dance. "Okay, Jerry." She clutched a cheap, beaded purse beneath her arm and walked from the table.

Andrews remained standing and watched her until she'd disappeared out the door.

Some part of him he hadn't suspected existed wanted more than anything to follow her.

Back in his room at the Hayes, Andrews sat restlessly on the sofa, his stockinged feet propped up on the coffee table. Leola Raymond's features, her subtleties of speech and movement, remained fixed on the dark screen of his mind. She should not have appealed to a U.S. senator serving on several influential committees, but she appealed to Jerry Andrews. Was this another Jerry Andrews, this man who slept in a cheap hotel and walked in the footsteps of a maniac's imagined men? Was he now, in somewhat the way of those whose lives he probed, a product of his own imagination? Or was it the other way around? Would the real Jerry Andrews please stand up? Step forward? Admit it?

Andrews laughed aloud at his rambling, inane thoughts. Might the authorities have the figment of Karpp's imagination imprisoned in the Belmont sanitarium? Once one impossible premise was accepted, other disturbing possibilities rushed in.

Andrews tried to push Karpp and Leola from his mind and think about Pat Colombo. Pat was special, as was Leola, and was in many respects not what one would expect as a senator's lady. It comforted Andrews to think about Pat, to construct her image lovingly, perfectly, in his memory. Dark brown hair and eyes, slightly overweight in breast and hip, smooth-skinned and lush, a bit too much hair on her arms, the very slightest trace of a mustache above her full, mobile lips, a natural, timeless grace that was more than elegance of movement. If she had a dozen kids she would love them all and be patient with them. If she sang, it would be soprano and with fine clarity and beauty. Pat Colombo. Right now, Andrews loved her, he was sure.

He decided to go downstairs for a quick supper, then he would return to his room and phone her.

17

Harry Jennings left the Bayon Lounge for his supper break. He was due back on duty behind the bar at nine o'clock, when the place started to fill with regular customers and the flow of tourists sampling Times Square and theater district night life. Jennings always ate at the same place, Farrota's Pizzeria over on Eighth Avenue. Angelo Farrota would know he was on his way and would have placed the pizza with the extra portion of black olives in the oven for him by now. Jennings had only to cut through the alley between Seventh and Eighth to emerge less than half a block from Farrota's.

The evening had started off merely cool, but now was becoming much colder. An icy drop of rain spattered against Jennings' lower lip. He licked it off, feeling it become warm on his tongue. The streetlight down the block illuminated only a very slight drizzle, so Jennings wasn't worried about getting wet.

As he turned into the dark alley leading to Eighth Avenue, he could almost smell the spicy aroma of pizza crust, sizzling tomato sauce and mozzarella cheese. He grinned. What he more likely smelled were the mingled overripe odors of the row of trash cans along the blank brick wall to his left. But damned if the effect wasn't the same. His appetite was fooled.

There was a slight scuffing sound ahead of Jennings, a leather sole scraping concrete. He stopped, breathing rapidly as he strained to see into the cool night. He realized with a New Yorker's ingrained caution that this was a perfect spot for a mugging.

One of the dark shadows on the wall before him moved, disengaged itself from the flat brick surface and walked toward him.

"Harry, it's me," the thing said.

"Holy Christ!"

Jennings' mouth opened again several times, wordlessly.

Something struck him on the side of the head, glanced off his shoulder. The ground beneath him swung away and he dropped into fearsome blackness.

18

"Where are you calling from?" Pat Colombo asked Andrews.

"I'm at the Hayes Hotel in Manhattan."

"I know the place," she said. "It's not your usual style."

Andrews settled back into the pillows he'd propped against the headboard, taking care not to get the cord to the receiver tangled. "I want to talk to you," he said. "Do you have time?"

She picked up the need in his voice, as he'd thought she would. "Don't be an ass," she said. "Talk."

So Andrews did talk, telling her everything about what had led him to Manhattan and the trail of Dana Larsen, and to the trails of the past lives of Martin Karpp. And he told her everything that had happened to him since his arrival here. Of his fear and sense of outrage upon finding that his room had been entered and Larsen's notes stolen. Of his increasing, haunting uneasiness.

"Go to see this Captain Franks," she said, when he was finished.

"Franks doesn't view things the way I do," Andrews explained. "And he has his job to consider. Priorities."

"But things have happened since you last talked to him."

"Nothing that constitutes hard evidence," Andrews told her.

"What about Dr. Larsen's notes being stolen?"

"I can't prove that they were. And remember, I took them

from Dana Larsen's apartment without permission."

There was a pause while the distance between phones crackled and hissed in Andrews' ear.

"Do you want me to come there and be with you?" Pat Colombo asked.

"No, I don't," Andrews said with slow deliberation. "But I wanted you to offer."

She laughed softly, almost bringing the receiver to life in Andrews' hand.

"What I want," he said, "is for us to be at the cabin, skiing in the daytime, making love at night, then sitting in front of a fire with some brandy-laced coffee."

"I've been thinking a lot about that myself, Jerry," Pat told him. "We'll get there."

He didn't say anything.

"Jerry?"

"Yeah?"

"See Franks."

"I love you. You're a touch of reality."

"Will you see Franks?"

"I will."

"Promise?"

"Do I have to?"

"Not to me. Not anything. Not ever."

Amos Franks ushered Andrews into his office, motioned with a sweep of a huge blue-sleeved arm for him to sit in the single chair near the desk, then sat down himself in a wood swivel chair that seemed too small to support his bulk. Franks had put on at least thirty pounds in the past five years. The massive police captain was now carrying far in excess of two hundred and fifty pounds on his six-foot-plus frame.

Franks drew a large, greenish cigar from his shirt pocket. "Senator?"

"No, thanks," Andrews said. "It looks poisonous."

"It is," Franks said seriously. He fired up the cigar with an ancient-looking silver lighter, then exhaled a great deal of smoke, as if he hoped Andrews would be gone when it cleared. Andrews wasn't.

"I guess this is about the Larsen case," Franks said in a resigned voice.

"I'm not sure enough that his death was accidental," Andrews said.

"Why not?"

Andrews told Franks about how there had been nothing concerning Martin Karpp in Larsen's office files, and about how the notes on Karpp were hidden in the golf bag. And he told him about his conversations with the people Dana Larsen had talked to regarding Karpp. Finally he related how the notes he'd taken from Dana's apartment had been stolen from his hotel room at the Hayes.

"You think somebody lifted the Karpp file from Larsen's office?" Franks asked.

"Of course. They didn't get the notes there because he'd hidden them. They were important."

"Why?"

"To Dana, because they represented a lot of work. I don't know why they were important to somebody else."

"The same somebody who took them from your hotel room?"

"It seems reasonable to assume so," Andrews said acidly.

"Unless it was a maid or a bellhop with a passkey, or you simply mislaid the notes."

"God damn it, Amos!"

"I'm telling you the way I have to reason on this, Senator. If you had any idea the kind of people we *know* are walking around out there, you'd see my point. You've brought me nothing hard, nothing new that I can act on."

"Are you telling me you still think Dana Larsen's death was an accident?"

"It's not what I think that matters, Senator. That was the finding at the inquest."

Andrews was stunned. "What . . . ?"

"There was an inquest. The finding was accidental death."

"Does that mean it's over as far as the police are concerned?"

For the first time, Amos Franks wavered. "No . . . If there's a reasonable suspicion that a crime has occurred, the case can be reopened." He puffed on the greenish cigar, then he stared, almost with fascination, into its glowing tip. "You ever read a medical textbook, Senator? You know how pretty soon you can start imagining you've got some of the symptoms? It can be that way when a friend dies—everything can appear suspicious if you let it get to you." He took another puff on the cigar, exhaled slowly and gazed off into the grayish haze that was polluting the office. "It'd be a good idea if you stayed in touch with us while you're in the city," he said.

"And it would be a good idea if you told me if and when you learn anything new on Dana Larsen's death."

Franks raised his eyebrows and a wary, angry glint appeared in his eyes. "Are you using your clout, Senator?"

"Of course not, Amos. It's just that I feel there's more to this than you do. I understand your position." Andrews was trying hard to placate the man. He didn't want to lose Amos Franks as a friend or an ally. "Here, you've got the clout,'" he added.

"I'm not a U.S. senator," Franks said.

"You should be glad."

"I am. Sure you don't want a cigar?"

Andrews laughed. "Not one of those." He extended his elbows and pushed up out of his chair.

"Senator," Franks said, "there's something else. Won't hurt for you to know it." It was amazing how little his broad, polished mahogany features gave away, despite their wide range of expression. "You mentioned Harry Jennings, the bartender at the Bayon Lounge. Jennings is dead, the victim of a hit-and-run."

Andrews sat back down.

"I didn't say murder, Senator," Franks said in a cautioning voice. "The man was struck by a car, that's all we know."

"There must be a connection," Andrews said.

"Maybe not."

"Only maybe?"

"There's nothing definite," Franks said, "except I got a caseload it'll take me a year to catch up on."

Andrews felt a cold vacuum of fear deep in his bowels. "What are the particulars of Jennings' death?"

"I don't know. I haven't read the report."

Andrews sat quietly.

Franks groaned and rose slowly from his chair. "All right, Senator." He left the office and returned a few minutes later with a pale-yellow file folder. After settling again into his undersized desk chair, he propped a pair of half-moon glasses on the bridge of his nose and read.

After a while, he said, "Nothing unusual for an H and R, Senator. Jennings' body was found in an alley near where he worked. The M.E. says he had a fractured sternum and died from internal hemorrhaging. There was some broken headlight glass near the body."

"What was Jennings doing in the alley?" Andrews asked.

"He used it as a shortcut to the restaurant over on Eighth Avenue where he usually ate supper. This time somebody in a car was using the alley as a shortcut at the same time."

Andrews stood up, shoved his fists into his pockets and began to pace in a tight, regular pattern. "Doesn't it seem like too much of a coincidence, Amos? I mean, first Dr. Larsen, now Jennings."

"People say that about the witnesses in the John Kennedy

assassination," Franks said patiently. "As if they expected all those folks to outlive everybody else. People die, is all. Always have and always will."

"Sooner or later, sure!"

"Well, in a way that's fifty-fifty, Senator. And two people with some connection to Martin Karpp died sooner rather than later. Think of how many people with Karpp connections are still alive."

Andrews stopped pacing and sighed. "Put that way, it sounds reasonable," he admitted.

"Don't make any difference how it sounds," Franks told him. "We've got to go with what we know. What you've told me, well, it borders on the supernatural. And a police board of inquiry's not superstitious, not even open-minded about such things. But like I said, if we do learn anything more, I'll let you know. So long as there's reciprocity."

Andrews grinned. "There will be, Amos. That's my profession."

On his way back to the hotel, Andrews stopped at the Korvettes on Sixth Avenue and bought a "burglarproof" lock from the hardware department. The lock consisted of a telescoping steel bar that could be wedged tightly between the base of the doorknob and the floor. A clerk assured Andrews it would make forcing the door open virtually impossible unless it was first reduced to splinters.

When he'd returned to his room, Andrews saw that the paper match he'd left between door and frame was undisturbed. He entered and tried the metal brace bar on the door. There was no way to test it from the hall side, but he was sure it would protect as advertised. When it was angled into position, the door might as well be another section of wall.

Andrews left the steel bar against the door. With it in place, he felt an almost womblike seclusion and security.

And after learning of Jennings' death, he felt an increased resolve to follow through with what he'd begun. The familiar subdued rage was in him, the rage he often felt when he saw people being used and abused, suffering unfairly under the imposition of someone else's will. He'd often mused that the feeling could be equated with social conscience and that it was the thing that had led him into politics. He hoped so. It was comforting to be able to ascribe such noble motivation to oneself.

He crossed the quiet room, sat on the bed and fished in his pocket for the scrap of napkin on which Leola Raymond had scrawled her phone number. He found it, unfolded it carefully and dialed.

"Jerry," Leola said tentatively, when he'd identified himself, "I was hoping you'd call. I wanted to talk to you."

"About Martin Karpp?"

"Well, yes, sure." A note of bewilderment and fear had edged into her voice, making it an octave too high. "I mean, about L.C. I saw him last night."

A coating of ice seemed to form around Andrews' heart. "What do you mean, you *saw* him?" It came out as if he were angry rather than alarmed.

"I mean when I was dancing at the Metropole, I looked out and there he was. He was turning away, starting to walk out, but I know it was him."

"It's dim as hell in there," Andrews said. "How can you recognize anyone for sure from up there with those spotlights blinding you?"

"They don't blind you. I'd recognize L.C., even from the back. Believe me."

Andrews did believe her. That was his problem.

"It's impossible, Leola." He didn't sound convincing and he knew it.

"So tell me I was hallucinating." Fear was making her sarcastic, as it had Andrews.

"Can I see you?" he asked. "I want to talk with you some more about this. And about some other things."

"Not now," she said. "Tomorrow morning's the earliest it's possible. Real early."

"Eight o'clock?" Andrews figured that would be real early to Leola.

"Better make it nine," she said.

Andrews smiled as she gave him her address.

"You be careful, Leola," he told her.

"Careful of L.C.? That's not necessary. It's just sort of creepy seeing him when it shouldn't be."

"That's the point," Andrews said, "it shouldn't be."

He hung up the phone and lay on his back on the bed, his fingers laced behind his head. Another unprovable to add to the sequence of unexplainable events. "Creepy," Leola had said. That was how Andrews felt. Creepy. He hadn't felt this way with such intensity since he was a child.

Andrews lay staring at the peeling paint on the old, high ceiling and wondered what a U.S. senator was doing here, sprawled on the bed in a decrepit hotel room and experiencing a child's fears. Maybe we never outgrow those fears, he thought, just carry them around with us in what we think is a safe place. Maybe, like Martin Karpp, we all contain more selves than we care to recognize.

A distant police siren singsonged outside, signaling someone else's desperation, making little impact on the collective consciousness of the crowded city.

Andrews felt like phoning Pat Colombo again, but he didn't.

Andrews continued to talk with the people who had known or had some contact with Karpp in his various identities. Friends, landlords, bartenders and fellow employees, lovers and haters, sympathizers and those who felt betrayed by Karpp's involuntary duplicity. Some of these people Dana Larsen had talked to. Most of them he hadn't.

The information Larsen had begun to compile, Andrews

expanded. There were long lists of habits, hangouts, acquaintances and marked peculiarities of L. C. Chambers, Jay Jefferson, Willy Bennet, Alan Hobson, even Karpp himself. Each personality seemed, while often diametrically opposed to another, to be supportive of some of the other personalities. Intriguing also was the way Karpp occasionally had talked of one or more of his other personalities to friends, who never dreamed that Karpp was in truth talking about his corporeal self. Karpp, or whoever he happened to be at the moment, knew, of course. There was too much evidence of existence left behind by his various selves for him not to know. And apparently more and more often he remembered the specifics of what he did as those separate selves.

Gradually Andrews was gaining insight into the splintered agony and multifaceted evasions of Martin Karpp. And he was becoming, for reasons imprecise to him, increasingly fascinated and fearful.

19

Vincent Grammo locked the door to his electronics shop, then pulled down and locked the steel mesh guard of the sort that most New York merchants use to discourage theft. He glanced up at the night sky, visible in a rectangular patchwork above the building tops, and saw no stars. He sniffed rain in the air, so he hurried toward his subway stop. Better to wait underground in the emptiness of the station than to be caught in a shower. He was sure it wasn't quite cold enough to snow.

This was influenza weather, the time of year he hated. He turned up his collar as he walked, sidestepping puddles as if they were perilous pits.

Within five minutes Grammo had descended to the tiled cavern of the station, purchased his token and pushed his way through the turnstile. There were three other passengers waiting for the subway. One was a down-and-out-looking man in a ragged red jacket. The others appeared to be like Grammo, businessmen heading home late after a rough day trying to stay afloat in the heavy seas of taxes, high interest rates and entangling government regulations.

The approaching growl of the subway sounded from the dark distances of the tunnel. A faint vibration played beneath Grammo's soles and he instinctively leaned forward to see the train.

116 /

It was on him quickly, and with a squeal and a hiss glided to a stop. Its doors slid open to allow admittance into the wide, brightly lighted cars. The car nearest Grammo was empty. He got in quickly, walked across the car to the uncomfortable plastic bench adorned with graffiti and gratefully sat down. His legs needed the rest, even after the short walk from the shop. He was past fifty now; age worked its mischief on a man with merciless, slow deliberation, toying grimly with the doomed.

As the train lurched into motion and accelerated, Grammo happened to glance out the window toward the platform he'd just left. His mouth fell open and he surprised himself with his own choked, startled cry.

For just an instant, before the platform had flashed out of sight outside the subway windows, Grammo had seen a figure standing near the turnstiles. A figure instantly familiar in its distinctive square-shouldered blockiness, strikingly eerie in its stillness.

For a moment Grammo had thought it was a man-sized cardboard cutout, an advertisement. But he knew it hadn't been that at all. He'd only hoped. The man had been wearing one of those flattish cloth caps, just as had Alan Hobson in the dead, deceptive past.

Grammo sat back and let the steady rocking of the car and the clacking of the rails soothe him. Metronome morphine. According to the percentages, even Vincent Grammo, worn down by time and molded by the pettiness of others, might have a near-perfect double, or at least one so similar that he'd be mistaken at a glance for Grammo. Especially if he wore some similar article of clothing. Say a certain kind of cap. That guy who'd been at the shop, Gerald Anderson, had planted ideas in his mind, that was all. Sometimes a person saw what he expected.

Still, Grammo might as well tell Anderson what—or who— he'd thought he'd seen on the subway platform. If Grammo could find the slip of paper with Anderson's scribbled phone number.

He would search for the number, but not very hard. It really wasn't that important, when he stopped to think about it. He didn't want it to be important.

The subway rushed on through its tunnel of blackness. Vincent Grammo picked up a folded *Times* someone had left behind and began reading about unexpected things that had happened to others.

20

Vincent Grammo had been home and asleep for hours when Leola Raymond arrived at her apartment after getting off work at the Metropole. She shut the door, sighed in breathless soprano exaggeration, and with a dancer's grace kicked off her shoes. They landed in darkness at opposite ends of the room. Her feet hurt, and she was hungry as well as exhausted. She reached for the switch to the secondhand floor lamp near the door.

The shabby apartment winked into illumination. It was messy: magazines scattered on the floor, dirty glasses standing like neglected chessmen on the coffee table, a noticeable layer of dust on the screen of the old black-and-white TV that received only two channels. Beyond an open doorway was an unmade bed, at the foot of which lay a bundle of unwashed clothes that Leola hadn't found the time to lug to the laundromat. Like many attractive women, she was sloppy with her belongings, fastidiously neat with her person.

She strolled with a smooth, splay-footed gait into the tiny kitchen, and by the light from the open refrigerator made a sandwich of bologna and mustard and poured some milk into a glass that she noticed for the first time was cracked. It took her only a few minutes to finish her snack, so she left the refrigerator door hanging open until she'd deposited the milk-filmed glass on the small drop-leaf table. Then she casually swung the door shut, transforming the kitchen from dim to dark, and walked toward the bathroom. The refrigerator clicked on and hummed behind her, as if trying to communicate some parting message.

In the bathroom, Leola deftly turned on the water in the tub, knowing from practice the exact position of the hot and cold faucet handles for a lukewarm mix. She unzipped her dress, let it drop to the floor and kicked it into a corner. Panty hose and panties came off next, then she sat nude on the cool edge of the tub and studied her feet. Her toenails needed polish again, and hard ridges of callus were forming along the edges of her insteps and her heels. A girl had to take care of her feet, especially in a job like Leola's. She stood up, got an emery board from the medicine chest, then sat back down and idly began filing her calluses. After her bath she would repaint her toes. If she wasn't too tired. She remembered that Jerry Andrews—Senator Jerry Andrews—was due here at nine the next morning—rather, later this morning. She stopped filing and absently ran her fingertips along the inside of a bare thigh. Andrews was kind of stimulating in a going-to-gray sort of way.

Leola tossed the emery board up onto the washbasin and watched with disappointment as it teetered and dropped onto the discolored linoleum floor. She knew that by now the tub would be filled to the proper level, so she stood, bent over and rotated the faucet handles until the rushing jet of water was reduced to a twisting trickle that quickly disappeared.

She stepped into the tub and lowered herself gradually, scooting her buttocks down on the smooth porcelain until the warm water reached her armpits. Leola moaned almost sensuously as her exhausted body, which had danced relentlessly through most of that evening, responded to the encompassing, penetrating warmth. Her muscular right leg twitched involuntarily as it relaxed.

Leola was reaching for the soap when she thought she

heard a soft creaking sound from outside the bathroom, a sound that momentarily made her bath water seem cold. Frantically she tried to remember if she'd bolted the hall door. Her memory played back conflicting versions of her entrance into the apartment. She sat very still, as if posing for an elegant nude portrait, listening, listening . . .

She heard nothing.

"Hello?" she called, in a voice whose loudness sprang at her.

After almost a full minute of silence, she let out a long breath and reached again for the soap.

Then the angle of light subtly changed in the bathroom. She knew without looking that the door had opened.

When she did look, she immediately recognized the moment she had dreaded.

"Oh, God, make it quick at least!" she said, and pressed herself back and up against the surface of the tub, so that if at all possible her hair would remain unmussed.

At five minutes to nine, Andrews knocked on the door to Leola Raymond's apartment and got no response. He decided to wait until exactly nine o'clock before either leaving or knocking more loudly. Leola might be getting dressed, or she might have stepped out. Andrews leaned against the wall opposite her door and began whistling tonelessly under his breath.

A door down the hall opened, and an obese woman wearing red boots and a tentlike yellow coat walked toward Andrews on her way to the stairs. As she drew nearer, she glowered at him as if questioning his presence and warning him that she would stand for no nonsense.

Andrews, feeling suddenly awkward and as out-of-place as she implied, gave her a reflex rigid smile meant to put them both at ease. "I'm looking for Miss Raymond," he said. "You wouldn't happen to know where she is."

The woman looked away from him and continued walking. He heard the wooden stairs strain beneath her passage as she descended out of sight. Far below Andrews the front door opened with a blast of rushing air and noise, then closed again to silence, like the airlock of a spaceship. He decided to knock again on Leola's door.

Still no response. Maybe she was still deep in sleep, unable to hear. Andrews did have an appointment for nine o'clock. He glanced again at his watch, knocked three times with increasing loudness. Then he tried the door.

Unlocked. He entered, calling Leola's name, and then closed the door behind him.

The apartment was a mess, a silent, apparently vacant jumble of dirty dishes, strewn magazines and discarded articles of clothing. Housekeeping obviously wasn't one of Leola's accomplishments.

"Leola?" Andrews' voice seemed muffled in the sunny, coldly silent apartment. He could see the bed in an adjoining room, unmade and empty. She must have gotten up. He took a few steps, looked into the kitchen. More dirty dishes, the remains of a TV dinner that might have been days old. He walked to another door and opened it. It was to the bathroom.

For a minute that was hours long, Andrews stood numbly in a rictus of revulsion and stared. Leola was sitting up in the bathtub, her lips barely parted, her eyes half open and glistening in the sunlight quietly blasting through the shadeless opaque window. On the linoleum beside the tub was what looked like a rust-stained razorblade. The water in the tub was thick and red, and it was its stillness and the stillness of the startlingly pale Leola that was horrible. She reminded Andrews of some terrible morsel grotesquely half-submerged in cherry Jell-O.

Bile rose in a bitter rush to the back of his throat and he turned away, staggered from the bathroom. He leaned over and supported himself on the back of the sofa with trembling outstretched arms, using all his willpower to keep from vomiting. He stared at his hands, concentrating on every tiny mark and contour of flesh, and let the vivid image of what he'd just seen fade around the edges until it was bearable.

Then he went to the telephone and called Amos Franks.

"It isn't suicide," Andrews told Franks, after Leola's body had been removed. "It was made to look like it, but she didn't kill herself."

Franks was making some final notations in a leather-covered note pad. "You might be right," he said. The fingerprint man finished and left, waving a casual goodbye. Franks and Andrews were alone now. "Know where he's hurrying off to?" Franks asked.

"Where?"

"Lunch."

Andrews stared at him.

"I mention that to help put this thing in perspective," Franks explained. "You're not used to violent death, much less the kind of violent death that leaves loose ends. We are."

"You're not telling me you're going to call this a suicide, are you, Amos?"

"Nope. Too much coincidence now. But I am telling you we're not going to rule out suicide."

"What about a note?"

Franks appeared pained. "What note? You think all suicides leave a note so things will be tidy for us? It's not that way, Senator."

"Three people involved with Martin Karpp have died within the space of two weeks."

"Which is why we're going to start digging," Franks said, "even though we don't have much of a shovel. And which is why you should go back to Washington, Senator."

Andrews grinned with realization. "It would be too big a coincidence if I were killed, wouldn't it?"

Franks nodded. "If there is something going on here, that might be precisely why you haven't been killed. The death of a U.S. senator would make big, big waves. A doctor, a bartender, a topless dancer, they make ripples. Ripples don't last as long or reach as far as waves. Ripples don't swamp boats."

"Then I'm safe. Why should I return to Washington?"

"Because you're less safe every day. They can't let you snoop around very much longer."

"They?"

"If there is a they. I never was much of a believer in the conspiracy theory. I've seen people killed on the spur of the moment over a stolen parking space."

"What about Martin Karpp?"

"What about him?" Amos Franks asked, irritated. "He's either here or he's there. Just because some bare-titted bimbo claims she saw him last night doesn't mean he's here in the city. On the other hand, the fact that he's under lock and key in a maximum-security institution means he *isn't* here in the city."

"She wasn't what you said, Amos."

Franks couldn't keep a dull gleam of surprise from his eyes. "All right, Senator."

"And she saw him. She ought to recognize a man she's been to bed with!"

"Don't bet on that," Franks said. "She was mistaken, Senator. That's all there was to that. Because that's all it could have been."

"Amos," Andrews said, "I like you and respect your ability, but there are certain well-traveled and restrictive channels to your reasoning."

"Fish don't fly," Franks said, "and if they could, I bet they wouldn't swim so well."

Andrews walked to a window and stared out at a weathered brick wall beyond the dark iron railing of a fire escape. What Amos had implied was true: the very thoroughness and reliance on firm facts that made him good at his job worked against him in something as vague and unusual as what was happening. He had only grisly results to work with, signposts to nowhere. The victims in question were not unlike hundreds of other victims he'd seen during the course of his career. Andrews could expect bureaucratic competence and sympathy from Amos, nothing more.

But Andrews did know someone who could both swim and fly. And burrow.

He said goodbye to Franks and walked out of the death-tainted normalcy of Leola Raymond's apartment. As he left the building, he expected to see some of the other tenants in the halls or gawking from behind partially opened doors. But the halls, and the sidewalk in front of the building, were empty. In this neighborhood, no one was interested. They had already begun to forget Leola Raymond.

21

~~~

"I don't see why you can't forget about it," Millikin said to Ellen Andrews as they sat in the restaurant of a secluded Maine lodge and sipped cocktails. They weren't staying at the lodge, but at a luxury motel whose owner was a longtime friend of Millikin's. Outside the vast window beside them, the Atlantic rolled in wrinkled white lines and undulating planes of murky green. The motif of the restaurant was Spanish. There were sombreros on the walls.

Ellen put down her strawberry daiquiri on its cork coaster and stared across the table at Millikin, as if unable to comprehend his reluctance to understand what she was saying. "First the man who lied about his appointment with Jerry," she said. "Then, I tell you, I'm sure I'm being followed. How can I forget it?"

Millikin gazed out to sea, as if really more interested in things that happened on water than on land. "Why would anyone be following you? There's no reason for Jerry to hire someone; we all know the situation."

"Do you think I'm imagining it?" Ellen asked. "Do you think I'm paranoid?"

"I love you because you're paranoid," Millikin said, still staring toward the indistinct horizon. It was one of those indecipherable remarks of his that sometimes distracted and irritated Ellen. A sort of verbal judo he practiced. Nobody ever got hurt, but she was always off balance, groping.

"I want us to go away," she said firmly. "I'm afraid."

Millikin turned his attention landward. "You? Afraid? But of what?"

"I don't know. That's why I'm afraid, naturally. That shouldn't be so difficult for you to understand."

"Good Christ!" Millikin said. He said it calmly but with emphasis. "You don't think anyone intends to harm you, do you?"

"Yes."

"Why?"

"Intuition. Mine is seldom wrong. I want us to go away, to Italy. To where we went before on the Ligurian coast."

Millikin finished his drink and signaled for another. "I don't know if I can do that, Ellen. I'm embroiled in an anti-trust case. Anyway, what would Jerry think? He was away himself the last time we were there."

"He wouldn't think anything even if he knew where I was. I'm not suggesting that we be gone for more than a few weeks. Jerry probably plans to spend his time with Pat Colombo."

"Are you sure he's still seeing her?" Millikin asked.

"He's involved with some woman. And they've been seen together lately. She's an editor for some financial magazine now, out of politics. But I'm sure it's the Colombo woman."

"Intuition again?" Millikin asked.

Ellen winced at the note of sarcasm in his voice. "It doesn't matter, does it, as long as I'm correct?"

"No," Millikin said. The waiter brought his drink and Ellen ordered another daiquiri. A very white gull soared in toward shore low and veered away an instant before striking the window. Millikin rested a hand on Ellen's wrist. "You really are frightened, aren't you?" he said, looking into her eyes as he had earlier looked out to sea.

She nodded, old in the harsh light reflected from the wide

sea and sky. From hidden speakers, grandiose and somber Spanish trumpet music began playing softly.

"I'll look into travel arrangements tomorrow," Millikin told her. He opened his menu and peered down at it as if it were some complex legal document, trying to ignore her gratitude. "Shall we try the flounder?" he asked.

"You know I don't like to dance," she said. She was young again, joking.

They laughed.

They were going away.

22

Andrews hadn't been able even to think of eating during the rest of the morning and afternoon. The image of the pale, dead Leola kept intruding in his mind, prompted by even the remotest stimuli. An old lady almost struck by a cab at an intersection: Woman: Death: Leola. A girl walking in front of Andrews, her only resemblance to Leola a high, artfully arranged mass of hair. Leola. The sight, the faint sound, of a topless bar on the other side of the street. Leola.

What Andrews did most of the rest of that day was walk. He had no particular destination, no direction. It seemed possible that by draining his physical strength he could also drain his memory of the dead woman, and perhaps drain the guilt that had settled like dark acid at the base of his mind. If he hadn't drawn Leola into the Karpp affair, she might be alive, might be at this moment dancing.

Andrews hurried across an intersection against the light and tried to convince himself that his contact with Leola might have made no difference. After all, it was Dana Larsen who had actually resurrected "L. C. Chambers" for her.

But wasn't it Dana Larsen whom Andrews had forgotten in the press of his work? Whose death he might have prevented?

But that, too, wasn't a certainty. Andrews walked faster.

Even here, in midtown Manhattan at nine in the evening, people were beginning to stare at him. He caught them glancing at him in the reflections of shop windows, from the windows of passing cabs and busses. Or was that also his imagination?

Probably not, he decided, realizing how fast and recklessly he was striding along the sidewalk, how stricken and grim was his expression.

He slowed, made himself relax as much as possible. His heart was hammering from his unconscious effort, and when he raised a hand it trembled unless he willed it to be still. Something in him, some other Andrews, had almost loved Leola Raymond.

He decided that he had to eat some supper, ingest something for his system to work on besides grief, guilt and frustration. For the moment, he'd forgotten fear.

Near the opposite corner on West Fifty-seventh Street was a small stand-up deli with a neon sign out in front that blinked EAT GOOD FAST. Andrews angled toward the window that advertised pizza by the slice, hamburgers, eggs any way, bagels and hot coffee. From the fierce, perspiring counterman, he bought a bagel and a large cup of coffee that was indeed hot. He found a spot at the crowded counter and set the paper cup down gingerly before it seriously burned his fingers. A tall, morose man in a rumpled blue business suit glanced at him and grudgingly sidestepped to give Andrews elbow room.

"I asked for a fuckin' large!" a voice argued behind Andrews. No one at the long counter seemed to hear, or if they did hear, to care how the disgruntled customer would come out in his disagreement with management.

Andrews ate slowly, chewing each bite deliberately before washing it down with a sip of the scalding coffee. When he was finished, the bagel seemed to have doubled in size and density in his stomach, but he felt better, stronger. The involuntary trembling of his hands had ceased. He finished his coffee slowly, added his trash to the overflowing contents of a container near the end of the counter and walked out.

He'd gone about half a block when he saw Martin Karpp.

Andrews was walking by the display window of a luggage shop when he glanced in, and there was Karpp staring back at him.

So startled was Andrews that he stopped and felt ice penetrate his bones. And so indistinct was the image of Karpp that he couldn't be sure if what he'd seen was Karpp inside the luggage shop, or Karpp reflected in the wide plane of the window.

Andrews spun and looked behind him, eyes darting searchingly up and down the street, across the street. There was no sign of Karpp. Andrews barged into the luggage shop.

"A sale on attaché cases today," a bespectacled clerk announced.

Andrews ignored him and ran to the shop's rear display area that afforded the only concealment for anyone inside. The only other customer, a young black man in jeans and a sport jacket, stared at him, then went back to examining the suede tote bag he was considering.

There was no one behind the racks of travel accessories at the rear of the shop. Accidentally knocking over a row of suitcases as if they were dominoes, Andrews hurried back toward the street. The bespectacled clerk glared at him with mild-mannered malevolence.

On the sidewalk, Andrews glanced about again, harboring no real hope of seeing Karpp. Had it been Karpp? Despite his indirect observation of the man, Andrews was positive he'd been looking at Martin Karpp. And yet . . .

Jangling the change in his pocket, Andrews charged into a phone booth on the corner. He was too curious even to wait until he'd returned to the hotel. He ensconced himself in the booth, armed with a handful of silver, and phoned Dr. Laidelier at the Belmont sanitarium.

Dr. Laidelier was still in his office. He listened to Andrews' request and clucked his tongue thoughtfully into the receiver, as if he might be considering Andrews for future residency.

"It's unusual, Senator," he said. "But there's no reason I can't check on Karpp myself, if you'll hold the line."

"I'll hold."

Andrews stood silently, his eyes constantly moving as he watched the thronging scene around the booth.

"Needless to say," Dr. Laidelier told Andrews, when he'd returned to the phone five minutes later, "Martin Karpp is right where he's supposed to be, where he's been since he was sent here."

"I saw him not ten minutes ago on West Fifty-seventh Street in Manhattan," Andrews said.

"Senator, with all due respect, that's impossible."

"You don't have to remind me." A sudden, wild thought struck Andrews. "Dr. Laidelier, does Martin Karpp have any brothers or sisters?"

"You mean a twin?"

"Even a brother who strongly resembles him."

"Sorry, Senator, Karpp was an only child. And thank God for that. You simply saw someone who resembled Karpp."

"It isn't likely I'd glimpse someone who so closely resembles him," Andrews said. "The same height and squarish shoulders, the same dark hair and thoughtful scowl."

"You did say glimpse," Dr. Laidelier reminded.

"I didn't get a chance to study him."

"And New York is a big city. Unless I'm lying to you, Senator, you couldn't have seen Martin Karpp. And I assure you I'm speaking the truth."

"I'm sure you are, Doctor. But . . . well, I can't come up with any explanations."

"I can't offer any, either," Laidelier said, "except to suggest that what you saw was the manifestation of an overactive imagination. Not as unusual as you might suspect, Senator.

132 /

And certainly nothing to worry about unless it happens recurrently."

The last thing Andrews wanted was psychoanalysis over the phone. What really aggravated him was that Laidelier might be right. In fact, *had* to be right.

"I'm sorry to have bothered you, Doctor."

"That's all right, Senator. It really is."

Andrews thanked Dr. Laidelier and hung up.

When he stepped from the phone booth, he realized for the first time how exhausted he was from his day of tension and ceaseless, aimless walking. It had been the sort of day that could well bring on the hallucination Dr. Laidelier was sure Andrews had experienced. Andrews had to concede that point. And wouldn't he be the person least capable of judging whether he'd hallucinated?

Then he remembered that contemplative, intent scowl directed at him through, or in, the luggage-shop display window. Three-dimensional or two? Andrews really didn't know. So how could he be so gut-deep positive of what he'd seen? Positive of anything? In so many ways, the world seemed at last to be revealing its vacillation of fact and substance, to be becoming unreal.

Andrews began walking again, this time slowly and wearily, head bowed, in the direction of his hotel.

It had seemed to Ellen like a transfiguration by an act of magic. Millikin had been as good as his word. One day they were in Maine, the next they were here in Italy, unpacking in the tiny pink villa that overlooked a quarter mile of gently sloping beach and then the sea.

They had stayed at the villa here on the Ligurian coast the year before. It belonged to a man in Rome, an old acquaintance of Millikin's, and usually sat empty. As he had last time, the man refused to accept rent from Millikin. And, like last time, Millikin had insisted and paid generously in advance by wire. The man never asked why Millikin wanted the use of the villa or whether he would have someone there with him. Millikin told Ellen that the villa's owner was slowly dying of cancer and had no more use for the sun, which he claimed had caused his illness.

The interior walls of the villa were rough plaster, here and there marked with fine cracks that resembled a system of roads seen from high above. The furniture was draped with heavy black plastic that was folded and fastened to the floor with wide strips of brown tape. Near the window on the seaward wall hung a framed, yellowed newspaper photograph of a pretty, dark-haired woman receiving a loving cup from a smiling elderly man in a tuxedo. There was no accompanying text, and the woman's plain dark dress gave no hint of when the photograph was taken. She was young, possibly still in her twenties, with expectation in her eyes.

"How long can we stay?" Ellen asked. She felt safe now, as far removed from danger as she had ever been. An abrupt and complete change of scenery can affect the senses like that. Though she knew this, she gave in to the effect gladly. It was why she had come.

"Indefinitely, really," Millikin told her. "No one but the owner knows we're here, and he forgets he owns this place until a yearly bill from a hired man comes in for maintenance expenses."

The surf whispered sibilant reassurances to Ellen. She sat down on the plastic-covered bed and simply enjoyed no longer feeling the vague uneasiness, the dark anticipation, that had threatened to overpower her at home.

That's the way you wanted it, isn't it?" Millikin said, hitching his thumbs in the beltless waistband of his chino slacks and smiling at her. "Private and anonymous."

There was an Anglo-Saxon colony on this part of the coast, but not near enough to disturb them. Their nearest neighbor was half a mile away, an old Italian woman who lived in a yellow villa with an overgrown wild garden. Yet they could walk to the small town of Pescare and buy what supplies they needed other than their weekly grocery delivery. "Seclusion and convenience," Millikin had said.

Ellen smiled up at Millikin. "It's what I wanted," she told him. "Thank you."

Millikin shrugged smoothly, almost indifferently. He was always embarrassed to be thanked. Anyway, he knew from experience how Ellen would demonstrate her gratitude. He said, "Well, here we are," and began to walk in aimless patterns, glancing about. "Shall we uncover the furniture?"

Ellen was still smiling. "Let's uncover a few other things first," she said.

23

Andrews was nearing his hotel when without warning he was bumped to the side, off the walk and into the deeply recessed dark doorway of a travel agency that had closed for the evening. He barely avoided falling. The street was dim, with relatively few passersby. A mugging, Andrews thought immediately, clutching his upper arm and shoulder, where pain still throbbed. The man must have been wearing soft-soled shoes as he approached Andrews from behind and skillfully separated him from the rest of the pedestrians, from the rest of the human race. The sidewalk and street beyond the deep doorway might as well have been in another city.

The man advanced on Andrews from the shadows. Andrews sucked in his breath in a harsh, surprised gasp, phlegm rattling in the back of his throat. The bulky dark form moving toward him was familiar.

Martin Karpp!

The square shoulders were hunched slightly forward, and in his right hand was a pipe or a club of some sort, dangling loosely at his side. He made no sound as he drew nearer to Andrews, whose shoes seemed to be imbedded in hardened concrete. Andrews tried to speak Karpp's name, heard himself croak a pitiable exclamation of dread. Of all things, this surely was happening to someone else.

As the ominous figure's hand raised the weapon, the entranceway flared into white brightness near the sidewalk. Brakes squealed and voices argued loudly and with passion.

"Five eighty, I told you! This cab ain't no escalator you can jump on for a free ride!"

"An' I told you we was goin' the long way. You think you're gonna run up the fare on me? . . ."

Less than a yard from Andrews, the man with the weapon stood motionless and poised. Time hung suspended with his upraised arm.

Andrews emerged from his debilitating fright with a burst of expanding terror, a strength and quickness he didn't ordinarily possess. He sprang around his assailant, bouncing off the thick plate glass of the travel agency's window as if it were unbreakable resilient plastic. Something that felt like a hornet sting shot through the right side of his neck. He was out onto the sidewalk, wheeling to run in the direction of the arguing voices.

The cab was parked half a block away, its headlights glaring blindingly at Andrews. He shouted and sprinted for it and the two men standing quarreling beside it.

He was on them in seconds, seeing surprised, frightened faces. The cabby was a lantern-jawed man with a flattened nose, his recalcitrant fare a lean, youthful Latin.

"What the fuck?" the cabby said, taking a full step backward away from the lunging Andrews. The younger man said nothing, dancing away in a graceful sideways leap. Andrews stopped himself by slapping his hands loudly and painfully against the parked cab's front fender.

"Somebody tried to kill me!" he blurted out. "There in that doorway!"

Now that he had help, his fear had been transformed to rage; he wanted to retrace his steps with his newfound companions and crush the man who'd threatened him. His palms still tingled from their contact with the fender.

"We calla police!" the cabby said. "Hey! Where you goin'!"

The Latin youth was trotting down the sidewalk, looking back and grinning. He raised a middle finger in an obscene gesture, put on an impressive show of speed and disappeared around a corner.

The cabby took an impulsive step after him, then spat angrily into the street and turned back. "Five eighty he did me out of!" he said, almost in disbelief. Then he glowered at Andrews, as if Andrews had been in cahoots with the boy who had run rather than pay. His anger sought a new, more accessible direction. "So where's this goddamn mugger?"

"That doorway," Andrews told him.

Side by side, the two men advanced on the dark entrance. When they neared it, they swung wide so that they could look into it from the curb. All they saw was darkness. Andrews felt a cold jolt of fear. What if Karpp had a gun? Andrews and the furious cabby were easy targets.

Apparently that possibility never occurred to the cabdriver. He suddenly charged into the doorway and disappeared in the darkness. Swallowing a lump of fear as big as a tennis ball and just as fuzzy, Andrews hesitated, then took several uncoordinated steps into the nightmarish blackness after the cabby. Several onlookers had gathered now, so tentatively poised that they seemed on the verge of disappearing. But as Andrews moved off the sidewalk, he drew courage from their presence.

"Nobody," pronounced a voice from the void. "If he was here, he's gone now."

The bulk of the cabby detached itself from black shadow. Andrews involuntarily took a step backward.

"We get a cop," the cabby said, striding around Andrews and back toward his cab. "We report your muggin' attempt and the little bastard that welshed on his fare."

Andrews followed, holding his hand to the side of his neck to still the throbbing where he'd been struck. The wound had been numb until now. He knew the blow had nicked him on the meaty part of his neck; a few inches left or right and it would have been his skull or collarbone.

Even as the cabby began to chatter into his radio mike, a police car pulled to the curb behind the cab. Its cherry lights continued to revolve regularly, losing rhythm with the siren as it growled to silence. Red glare played over dark shadow, like paint of a different composition, never quite mixing. "Forget it," Andrews heard the cabby say. The radio in the police cruiser blurted out something loud, metallic and unintelligible.

A tall, angular cop approached Andrews and the cabby, who'd gotten out of his cab and walked around to the sidewalk.

"What's the story?" the cop asked.

"Fare skipped out on me," the cabby told him, not giving Andrews a chance to speak. But when it turned out that the sum lost was only five dollars and eighty cents, the cop turned his attention to Andrews.

"What happened to your neck?" he asked.

"Somebody tried to mug him," the cabby said. "Right there in that doorway."

Andrews told his story while the cop listened attentively and even sympathetically. An attempted mugging. What else could it have been? Andrews didn't argue.

"Description?" the cop asked.

"It was dark," Andrews said. "A stocky man, square-shouldered, silent when he walked."

The cop waited a few seconds, then looked up from the notes he was scribbling. "That's it?"

"Sorry," Andrews said. "It was dark," he said again.

"Did he get anything?"

"No."

"Ask for money?"

Andrews shook his head no.

"It'll have to be plain assault then," the cop said. "You see which direction he ran?"

"Down that way," the cabby said, pointing.

"The mugger?"

"No!" the cabby spat. "The kid! Maybe he's from the neighborhood!"

"Let me finish here and I'll be with you," the cop said calmly.

"I didn't see him come out from the doorway," Andrews said.

The cop looked around, raised his voice. "Did anybody see the suspect flee from that doorway?"

No one answered. Andrews wondered why cops always adopted the language of reports when speaking to the news media or public gatherings.

"Like always," the cop said. He slapped his notebook shut and peered with narrow blue eyes at Andrews' neck. "You want hospital treatment?"

"It's not that bad," Andrews said.

"Not much hope to catch the guy," the cop said. "Happens like this too often. You from out of town?"

"Washington, D.C."

"Just as bad there, I hear."

"A different kind of stealing," Andrews told him.

The cop grinned and nodded, a veteran of the lower, more visible echelons of corruption. "Call us at the Seventeenth if you think of anything else, Mr. Andrews. Anything comes up on our end, we'll phone you at the Hayes if you're still in town. You here on business?"

"Yes, for a few weeks."

"Well, sorry this had to happen. But don't hope too hard to hear from us."

Andrews said that he wouldn't and watched the cop stroll back toward the parked cruiser. The cabby hurried to catch up with him.

"This'll be an hour's wages outa my pocket while I go fill out a theft of services report!" Andrews heard the cabby say, beginning to raise his voice in indignation as he waved his arms. The cop was listening tolerantly, obviously eager to get back into the quiet of the police car.

Andrews brushed past the few onlookers still standing silently nearby. He walked on toward his hotel. He stayed as near as possible to the curb, well away from the blackness of recessed doorways and narrow alleys.

In his room, Andrews stood shirtless before the bathroom mirror and twisted his neck so he could see the area of scraped skin that was beginning to darken to a bruise. The neck was stiff now, as if he had exercised too strenuously an hour ago and the muscles were cramping. He ran some hot water on a washrag, folded it and walked to the bed as he held the warm compress to the wound.

Andrews lay wearily on the mattress and tried to sort out what had happened. Had it been merely a mugging attempt? He doubted it. And despite his limited vision in the dark doorway, the figure that had attacked him was built like, even seemed to move like, Martin Karpp. Andrews could hear Amos Franks asking him how many times he'd seen Karpp. "Once," Andrews would have to answer. But Andrews knew better.

He thought back to the attack in the doorway and his escape. Everything had happened so swiftly, was so disjointed in memory. Had Karpp had time to run from the doorway without being seen? Andrews simply couldn't recall. Time didn't move in measured sequence during such a crisis.

And if Karpp hadn't had time to escape from the doorway, where *had* he gone? Had he even been there? The steadily pulsing pain in Andrews' neck and shoulder told him that someone had been there.

He sat up on the mattress, stacked the pillows behind his back and leaned against them, trying to hold his head and neck still. Switching hands on the folded, gradually cooling washrag, he pulled the phone from the bedside table and rested it in his lap. Then he dialed direct to CIA Headquarters in Langley, West Virginia, using a number he'd been supplied with several years ago, and identified himself.

After some expected delay, he was told where and when he could get in touch with Sam Underwood.

24

Judy Carnegie finished dressing and poured herself a cup of coffee from the electric pot on her kitchen counter. She kept the pot plugged into a timer, and each morning she awoke to the gentle gurgling and pungent aroma of perking coffee. Not only did that system save valuable time in the mornings, but it provided a daily incentive to rise. Unlike most energetic, ambitious people, Judy Carnegie could sleep away the day if nothing roused her.

But she had uncommon incentive to get out of bed early today. Work was stacked up at the office higher than it had ever been. It would have been so much easier all the way around if the senator had stayed in town for at least a week to help her. The only consolation was that Judy could work undisturbed in his absence. What she could accomplish by herself, she would get done without the usual interruptions.

She sat at the Formica table and sipped coffee while she idly scanned the *Post*. This was the daily initial ritual of her job. It was surprising how some seemingly innocuous bits of information, when juxtaposed with other data, could become suddenly meaningful.

But there really wasn't much in the way of news this morning. Not like in the Watergate years. Judy wondered what it would have been like to work in Washington during that unsettled era. Sometimes she regretted having missed it. She had an appetite and a talent for picking her way through chaos. That was why she complemented her boss. Andrews, easygoing and personable as he seemed, despised chaos, had learned to tolerate it only while trying to set it straight.

It was odd that he hadn't told her where he could be reached. That sort of thing usually wasn't done; the unexpected cropped up at just such times. "New York," was all he'd said. Judy was sure he wasn't going anywhere with Pat Colombo. He'd always informed her of that when it happened, needed her at times to run interference. New York. Maybe he was there with his wife. It struck Judy as absurd that Andrews might inform her of trysts with his mistress, yet keep it a complete secret if he wanted privacy with his wife. She smiled around the rim of her cup as she finished her coffee.

Someone else knew that Andrews was in New York. A man had phoned the office the day after he left and asked where the senator could be reached. Not only did the fact that the man knew Andrews was in New York strike Judy as odd, but he seemed dissatisfied almost to the point of anger when she'd told him she couldn't put him in touch with Andrews. And then he'd tactfully refused to identify himself.

But he had known Andrews' general whereabouts. Judy was undeniably annoyed by the knowledge that Andrews would confide in someone else to the same extent he'd confided in her.

She rinsed out her coffee cup and set it upside down on the drainboard. She was hungry, but she'd decided to skip breakfast as part of her attempt to shed the few pounds she had lately gained from her long hours of sitting, doing Andrews' research on the upcoming Senate confirmations. Avoiding even looking at the refrigerator, she left her apartment and took the elevator down to the basement garage where her two-year-old Mustang was parked.

A few minutes later, the immaculate yellow Mustang emerged from the shadows of the underground garage exit into bright, cold sunlight, made a sharp left turn and sprightly joined the swift morning traffic.

Judy Carnegie wasn't the type to look back, either in life or in driving. It never occurred to her that she might be followed.

Andrews was dreaming. He knew that was so even as he dreamed. That was all he knew. He was alone somewhere he had never been, aware of high, formless clouds, a rushing sound, softness that gave like flesh beneath his feet. The beach! But what beach and when he didn't know.

He rounded a corner of something looming and immeasurable and found himself facing the open sea. Several stars observed him like the eyes of night animals, their celestial arrangement unfamiliar in the black sky. And he was no longer alone.

Three figures were standing near the reaching surf, their arms at their sides. Andrews knew that they were waiting for him. The fleshiness began to move under his suddenly bare soles, carrying him toward the three figures faster than the length of his strides, yet with inexorable slowness.

When he was nearer, he saw by a grayish flickering light, much like the light cast by a film projector, the features of the three figures, and his heart spun crazily between poles of joy and fear. The smallest figure was Andrews as a youth of about twelve. The figure next to it was the same Andrews as a young man. The last figure was old, holding itself very, very erect, as if the weight of time might descend sparingly around it.

The three figures rolled eyes that were the same toward Andrews, said nothing, did nothing.

And passed to him an indecipherable certainty.

A dank and morbid dread enveloped Andrews, compressed heavily about him, suffocating him in chill and sickening apprehension. He looked to the sky, saw only blackness now and screamed noiselessly into it.

The muffled, ordinary sounds of the city told Andrews that he was awake.

Nightmare.

The dread remained with him. His heart was bucking against his ribs like a thing driven and unbalanced, and he was perspiring.

My God, he thought, wouldn't Freud have had fun with that? Or Fellini? Or Dana Larsen?

25

When Samuel Underwood walked into Andrews' room at the Hayes, he smiled and nodded but said nothing. It was Andrews who had phoned and set up the meeting.

Andrews invited his slender, tastefully attired visitor to sit, then offered a drink. Underwood sat down in an armchair that was beginning to show wear at the edges of the cushion, but he declined a drink.

"I need help," Andrews said flatly. He had known Underwood since Watergate and had a respect for the man's ability and candor. One day, Andrews was sure, Underwood would move up that remaining short climb in his career and become chief of the CIA. Discretion was his religion.

"I gathered that, Senator. What sort of help?"

Andrews snorted, suddenly struck by a dark humor. "Can you assign a bodyguard-detective-clairvoyant?" he asked.

"Sure, we have those." Unblinking gray eyes remained serious.

Andrews wondered for a moment if Underwood had meant what he said.

"Bothered by ghosts?" Underwood asked.

"More like doppelgangers."

"They bother us all." Underwood settled into his chair with exaggerated relish, as if he'd been playing a dull game that suddenly had turned interesting. "Give me the specifics," he said.

Pat Colombo leaned over the meat counter in the Boulder supermarket near her apartment and tried to outwit the grocer at his own game, juggling price and weight to determine if sirloin was cheaper than flank steak. Only lately had she begun to examine grocery prices carefully; unlike a certain senator, whom she happened to love, she couldn't vote herself a pay raise to keep pace with inflation. She wished at that moment that she were shopping for food that she and Jerry would share. She smiled at her womanly wiles. Gastronomical romance. She decided on the flank steak, picked it up and laid it gently in the bottom of her grocery cart, so that none of the juice would run from the styrofoam tray.

When she looked up she saw the thin blond man again.

He had walked into the supermarket behind her, then in the soup aisle she had glanced up to catch him staring at her. Now he was standing near a pyramid of canned potato chips, looking past the display at her with avid interest. When Pat returned the stare, he looked away, then sauntered toward Spices.

There were some men, she'd heard, who considered the supermarket an ideal place to make advances on women. She had to agree that in a way the theory was sound. Most women seldom dressed up to shop for groceries; what a man saw was what he'd get. And the blond man, not unhandsome in a gaunt, anemic fashion, might have enjoyed success with women in such a mundane setting. But he could expect no success with Pat, who was involved with Jerry Andrews and the problem of stretching her food budget.

She was worried about Andrews. His basic stability was the first thing Pat had noticed about him, and it was no illusion. Jerry Andrews, more than any man she'd ever met, knew who and where he was all the time. Yet what had happened in

New York seemed to have knocked the underpinnings from that stability, both in obvious ways and in ways that only a lover might notice even from a telephone conversation. There were disturbing nuances in the things he said and the way he said them. She hadn't mentioned to him the sudden sensation of unfamiliarity she'd experienced while talking with him on the phone, as if for an instant she had been speaking with a stranger.

As she checked out, Pat made it a point not to glance in the direction of the blond man. He was several counters over, in the express lane, juggling a six-pack of beer, several bags of pretzels and a gallon of milk while advancing on the register with half steps as the line moved slowly forward.

Pat paid the artificially cheery check-out girl, wheeled her two bags of groceries outside to her car and placed them in the trunk. She rolled the empty cart into a no-parking area marked off by yellow stripes on the smooth blacktop, then got into her car and started the engine.

The blond man was three cars behind her, at the wheel of an unobtrusive blue Ford, as she headed toward her apartment at a fast clip to reach home before the ice cream in the trunk became soft enough to run.

As he drove, the blond man hummed softly to himself, a patient man in a job that demanded patience.

26

Underwood had listened to Andrews' story with hardly a change of expression. His eyes seemed to be focused on some absorbing object above and beyond Andrews' left shoulder. But he'd been listening. When Andrews was finished talking, Underwood asked him several succinct questions in order to have the facts straight beyond doubt, then sat still as if quietly analyzing an opponent's intriguing chess move.

Andrews watched him uncomfortably, wondering if the CIA executive thought that a U.S. senator had slipped a mental cog and was posing a problem. Unable to endure the silence of the composed Underwood, Andrews finally said, "Any ideas?"

"If we're dealing with the supernatural," Underwood said, "of course there is nothing we can do." Andrews saw that Underwood was serious. "So we'll proceed on the assumption that we can deal with whatever it is that might be threatening you."

"Might? Three people connected with Karpp recently died. Surely you don't think, like Franks, that it's all a coincidence and no one death has anything to do with the others."

"I don't believe that, Senator. And, unlike Amos Franks, I don't have to wait for hard evidence on which to act. I can take action on even slight possibilities. You've given me possibilities more than slight, so there's no problem there." He shifted in the worn armchair and crossed his legs. Well tailored as he was, there was a dark, layered hole in the sole of his right shoe. "You're right," he said to Andrews. "You do need help." He stared hard at Andrews, then laughed softly. "Not psychiatric help, Senator."

Andrews couldn't help but feel relief. "I know how insane the story sounds," he said.

"It doesn't, really," Underwood replied. "It's like a code without a cipher. But every code can be broken."

"True enough," Andrews said. "But most codes need to be broken in time to prevent whatever it is they were devised to conceal."

"And that," Underwood stated with underlying steeliness, "is the job I'm best at: preventing. But of course you must pledge your cooperation."

"I didn't ask to see you in order to question your expertise," Andrews said. And already he felt safer in the presence of the cool, flawlessly professional Underwood. Together, using Underwood's know-how and long experience, perhaps they could untangle the knots and fears of the past week.

Underwood stood up, buttoned his suitcoat. "If you were planning on going out," he said, "don't. In a few hours, I'll want you to meet someone."

The someone Underwood wanted Andrews to meet was Nels Graham, another CIA man, but one about whom Andrews knew nothing. Graham was about fifty, sandy-haired, with one of those good-humored yet pugnacious Irish faces that usually are associated with smaller men. But Graham wasn't small. He was at least six foot four, and Andrews suspected that the man possessed an athlete's strength in his angular limbs. Twenty-five years ago, Graham would have looked right at home as a hard-driving playmaker on a college basketball team. He smiled a friendly, overgrown-leprechaun smile at Andrews. Then he reached to the side with a long arm and opened the door to the hall to admit another man.

"This is Robert Arlen, Senator."

Arlen shook Andrews' hand and smiled. He was about Andrews' height and build. He was leanly handsome, had dark hair just beginning to gray and symmetrical blue eyes that lent him a level, reasonable expression. Andrews saw the similarity immediately, but it was not so great that he thought it might be anything but coincidental.

It wasn't coincidental. "Mr. Arlen is going to be you," Underwood said to Andrews.

Andrews looked at the three men before him. They all wore much the same expression, one of professional nonchalance yet with an unmistakable subterranean spark of interest, like poker players nursing promising hands.

Andrews sat down in the worn armchair. "I see . . ." He looked up sharply. "It's ironic that our last names are vaguely similar. But he doesn't really look enough like me to fool anyone."

"Remember, Senator," Graham said, "you've been physically attacked. You're afraid now, not likely to show your face unless you have to. And after you fill us in for the next few hours, you'll be surprised at how strikingly Mr. Arlen can resemble you from a distance."

"And not a very long distance at that," Arlen said with what Andrews thought was too much confidence.

"Mr. Graham will be in charge of the operation," Underwood told Andrews. "He's run this sort of show before. You can have faith in his ability."

Andrews looked again at Nels Graham's almost devilish Gaelic countenance. Graham grinned down at him from atop his tall frame. It was an oddly controlled grin that conveyed a quiet imperturbability. Arlen merely stood with his hands folded before him, already studying Andrews.

"Where is the real me supposed to be while this impersonation is taking place?" Andrews asked.

"Where you were going to be in the first place, Senator," Underwood said. "That cabin in the mountains. It seems an ideal spot to have you safe and out of the way while we deal with the problem. And incidentally, we know about Miss Colombo, have for some time. Both of you are free to go on about your business as planned. It would be best that way."

Andrews didn't know whether to feel guilty or angry. He became aware that his fists were clenched. He unclenched them. Of course he'd always considered the possibility that Intelligence knew about his relationship with Pat. After all, they were both security-cleared to handle the most sensitive material. But he'd never expected it to come to a face-to-face, casual reference to his extramarital affair.

Underwood knew what Andrews was thinking. "You're among the cleanest of the clean, Senator. You'd be shocked if you read our files." The elegantly attired CIA man shrugged. His expensive suit shrugged like a second skin along with him. "That's the way it is, unfortunately, and it's better that we know."

Sometimes Andrews wondered about that, but he nodded in meaningless agreement.

Underwood looked at his watch. "Arrangements have been made to get you out of the city secretly. We'll depart in three hours. Until that time, I'll leave the three of you to the necessary conversation." He smiled at Andrews, glanced at Graham and Arlen without smiling, then left the room.

Every minute of the next three hours was utilized. Graham and Arlen grilled Andrews exhaustively on his activities since arriving in Manhattan, on his personal habits and manner of dress. Andrews learned that Arlen already had studied films of him that Andrews never knew existed. He surprised Andrews with an almost perfect imitation of the senator's long-striding, arm-swinging walk.

At five o'clock, Underwood returned. He was carrying a large paper bag full of folded clothes. He showed Andrews his reassuring smile. "You have fifteen minutes to pack, Senator." Methodically, he began arranging the clothing on the bed. There were slacks, shirts, a light-colored topcoat.

"They appear to be close to my size," Andrews said.

"They're your size exactly, Senator. They're to replace the clothes you're going to leave for Arlen to wear." He folded the now empty paper bag into fourths, then eighths, flattened it and stuffed it into his suitcoat side pocket. There was no bulge to disturb the lines of the coat. "Ten minutes now, Senator."

Andrews began packing.

"You're booked on a TWA flight to Pittsburgh under the name L. Akers," Underwood said. He held up a red-and-white TWA boarding pass. "Dinner on the plane." Then he moved his fingers sideways, like a card player spreading his hand, revealing another airline ticket behind the first. "In Pittsburgh you have a half-hour layover before a connecting flight to Denver. Then you're on your own, Senator—out of this mess."

"What if I'm followed?"

Underwood appeared remotely insulted. "You won't be. That I can guarantee."

Andrews latched his suitcase and spun the combination lock, zipped closed his folding garment carrier. He was packed.

Again Underwood stole a glance at his gold wristwatch. Time was the controlling factor in his life. He briskly crossed the room and stood by the open door, waiting for Andrews.

"Good luck, Senator," Nels Graham said.

Andrews thanked him, then looked at Arlen. "Good luck to you," he said to the man who was to take his place and align himself with danger.

Arlen nodded calmly. By some trick of the eye he was beginning to seem more and more a passable double for Andrews.

Andrews and Underwood rode a service elevator to the hotel's subbasement. After a wait of only a few minutes in damp dimness, Underwood led the way up a flight of narrow concrete steps to a door that opened into a delivery alley behind the hotel. A battered taxi was waiting. Andrews knew that the driver wasn't an ordinary cabby. Underwood held open the cab door for Andrews. The driver stared straight ahead as if he were alone, like a well-groomed mannequin from Macy's.

"He knows where to take you," Underwood said.

Andrews got into the cab, and Underwood closed the door almost silently and leaned forward. "There's no need for you to worry anymore, Senator," he said through the rolled-down window.

As the cab pulled away, he gave Andrews a smile and a jaunty little military half salute.

27

Ellen Andrews awoke to the sound of the sea. The windows were open, squares of speckled starlight between gently swaying sheer curtains. The open windows were the room's only source of illumination; it was much darker inside than out.

It was pleasant, Ellen thought, to lie comfortably in bed and be lulled by the primal rhythm of the surf. This was one of those crystallized instants of perfection in one's life. Ellen felt an almost sexual security and awareness. Here she was remote from her problems, warm yet with a gentle, caressing breeze playing over her thinly clad body, content for the moment, protected by the man who slept in the bed along the opposite wall, installed in the midst of starlighted beauty and soothed by the whispering rush of the sea.

But what had awakened her?

As Ellen lay in the darkness with her back molded to the mattress, she slowly became aware of another sound. It was a sighing, low gurgling, like yet unlike the sound of the surf that gently almost overrode it. Was it coming from outside?

Completely awake now, Ellen lay motionless and listened intently. She couldn't be sure of the source of the sound that persisted between the breaking of waves on the sand.

Then the sound stopped.

Ellen realized that the sound could have been made by Millikin. It had come from the direction of his bed. It was possible that he was sick. She decided to check on him to make sure he was all right. She was sure he would be, and that she would stay the rest of the night in his bed.

Carefully, gropingly, she crossed the dark wood floor and felt her right leg come in contact with Millikin's mattress. With outstretched arms, she reached like a blind woman, splayed fingers raking the down-turned sheet, the soft cool pillow. The bed was empty.

Ellen straightened and the darkness seemed to converge on her, bringing with it sudden fear that caused her heart to create the loudest sound in the still room. Or was the room quaking gently in time with her heart? She decided to call Millikin.

"Lawrence?" Her own voice was like the shock of cold water.

Millikin didn't answer. If he were anywhere inside, he'd have heard her. Ellen told herself without conviction that he might have been unable to sleep and stepped out for a smoke or a walk on the beach. But, to her knowledge, he'd never done such a thing before. Slowly, her arms extended forward like exploring antennae, she began traversing the dark room toward the light switch. Her bare feet were aware of every splinter or irregularity in the plank floor.

Her right big toe struck something soft, seemed for an instant that it might penetrate. She shrieked and leaped back.

Then, unable to do anything else in the blackness, Ellen forced herself to bend down and feel what it was she had prodded with her toe.

Her fingertips pressed into the flesh of a human midsection. She moved her fingers, felt coarse hair on the chest, was immediately aware of the stillness beneath her hand. "Lawrence!" she whispered.

She straightened when she heard movement behind her.

Someone was here in the room with her! God, someone was here!

"Who is it!" Her words were a stranger's choked sob.

Only the calm voice of the surf answered.

"Please! Who's there!"

In panic, she sprang toward the opposite side of the room, toward the light switch.

He was waiting for her there.

As her hand reached out and flipped the switch that transformed darkness to brilliance, something closed on Ellen's throat with unbelievable force. Her scream was inward, soundless, burning through every nerve in her body. The pressure on her throat loosened, tightened, allowing only a low, sighing gurgle. The writhing, weakening struggles of Ellen's body were involuntary, the reflex protest of a dying organism. She wanted it to end.

She died staring up with bulging, distorting eyes at a face she'd never before seen.

No one from the village knew where the Americans had gone. But then no one knew from where they had come. They simply had arrived, then left again without notice.

Antonio Biagio, the deliveryman who went for the regular grocery order, found that the tiny pink villa was empty, the American couple's few possessions gone. The next day, too, the villa was vacant. Antonio shrugged, and when he returned to the village he mentioned the Americans' absence to a few people at the cantina. Then he forgot the matter. There was nothing to be done about it.

Months would pass before the bodies would be found and identified.

28

The flight to Denver was no more eventful than any other flight Andrews had taken. The stewardesses smiled, the pilot soothed, the food was reprocessed plastic.

After retrieving his luggage, Andrews took a cab to a car-rental agency he usually dealt with when in Denver. The agency specialized in rough-terrain vehicles, four-wheel-drive Jeeps advertised able to go anywhere.

Al Kramer, the agency owner and operator, greeted Andrews and informed him that all but a few of his vehicles were rented. The only ones he had left were the high-powered, high-rental-fee Jeeps with cold-weather remote-control starting. Remote-control starting was a luxury feature that enabled the driver to stay in bed in the morning, start the Jeep with the press of a button, then later enter a nicely warmed-up vehicle that was comfortable and ready to go. The weather really wasn't all that cold in the mountains this time of year, so Kramer was stuck with these Jeeps until winter moved in seriously.

Andrews momentarily considered leasing a regular passenger car somewhere else. Reaching the cabin was no problem, but he and Pat liked to take a Jeep into rough country higher up the mountain, where they could climb and ski in total isolation. He told Kramer he'd take one of the remaining

Jeeps and arranged for payment with his American Express card. He would drive the seventy-five miles to the little town of Perith, where he would meet Pat, rent skis and buy supplies. Then they would drive up the winding mountain road to the cabin.

The Jeep was rough on the highway, and one of its headlights jiggled and was aimed at too steep a downward angle. Andrews kept his speed slow so he could see. He didn't mind the bouncing. It helped to keep him awake.

It was almost eleven o'clock when he turned the Jeep onto Perith's main street.

Perith wasn't much of a town, a section of ancient brick stores, a newer shopping strip built to resemble old brick, a corner where all four of the town's service stations (one of them boarded up) were located, a few taverns that catered mostly to natives. It was a town that lived in the shadow of the mountains, subsisting on faltering lumber and mining industries until, with the blossoming popularity of skiing, new money began to trickle in. When the snow was right, the mountains above Perith were excellent ski country.

Though Andrews skied, he regretted the increasing influx of tourists. He valued the cabin for its isolation, for the privacy and surcease it provided. And it had become, for Pat and him, one of those places that lovers make special.

He saw her red MG convertible parked in the lot of the Snow King Motel, a recently constructed U-shaped, two-story building with a restaurant, coffee shop and souvenir shop at one end. As Andrews parked beside the sports car, he saw Pat sitting near the window in the coffee shop. The Jeep's headlights had caught her attention. She waved to him as he leaned forward to switch off the engine.

The chill in the air surprised Andrews as he stepped down from the warm interior of the now mud-spattered gray Jeep. Perith was high above sea level, but usually warmer this time of year. Probably there would be plenty of snow up in the mountains.

Andrews kissed Pat lightly on the lips as he sat down opposite her. A white-aproned teen-age boy sauntered out from behind the counter and took his order for Nestlés hot chocolate. Pat was drinking hot chocolate topped with a swirl of whipped cream that rose to a point.

"I rented us a room here," she said. "Everything's closed, so we can't get supplies or skis until morning. Anyway, I didn't want us to have to drive that narrow mountain road in the dark."

Andrews told her that was fine, told her he loved her. His hot chocolate came and he sipped it tentatively, found it scalding. "Been here long?" he asked.

"About an hour. I didn't mind waiting."

Andrews let himself relax, realizing that for the past week he'd never been fully free from tension. The presence of Pat Colombo was working its customary white witchcraft, exorcising whatever demons plagued him.

"Want to tell me what's happened since you phoned?" Pat asked.

"Christ, not now. I don't even want to think about it."

"Then you shouldn't," Pat told him. "There's no need to."

"Oh, there's a need. I just don't want to face it for a while."

Pat lifted her hot chocolate and slowly but deftly licked some of the cream from the rim of the mug. It was not a deliberately seductive gesture, but it sent a persistent pressure along Andrews' groin and quickened his heartbeat. Pat's face was slightly flushed from the cool air, her dark eyes bright and alert despite the long drive and late hour. She was one of those women in whom health and sexuality are almost synonymous.

"It's you I want to think about now," Andrews told her. "And nothing else."

Pat stared directly at him with eyes that held no deviousness, no inhibition. "Do you want to finish your chocolate?" she asked.

"No."

"Good."

Andrews signaled the teen-age boy for the check.

She was a revelation and a renewal. She always was. Andrews lay next to Pat Colombo and wondered if in their lifetime he ever could become bored with her. He doubted it; he really did.

In the motel's king-size bed, by the light of the flickering and silent TV, he was comforted by the pressure of her sated, warm body against his as he brought her up to date on what had happened in Manhattan. It all seemed so far removed now, a madness that involved other people.

"Suppose you were followed here," she said, when he'd finished talking and dropped his head back onto the soft pillow.

"You have to assume that the CIA knows what they're doing," Andrews said. "That's not so difficult to do if you know Underwood."

"But you said a man named Graham was in charge of the . . . operation."

"That's what the CIA calls it," Andrews said. "Real-life spy terminology. Graham's in charge of details; he's Underwood's man." He turned onto his side and kissed her, running his hand along the silken arch of her back.

"Have you ever read the theory that successful men in politics are supposed to have overdeveloped sexual libidos?" she asked.

"Yes, and it's true," Andrews said.

"It's also true that I'd like to be able to get out of bed and walk tomorrow."

Andrews laughed and released her. He got up, put on his underwear and pants and walked to the bucket of ice cubes they'd gotten from the machine in the hall. He dumped the diluted remains of his last drink from his glass, then put in fresh ice and two fingers of the Chivas Regal that Pat had brought for him.

Then he turned to face her, watching the soft play of light from the TV screen cast varying shadows over her smooth flesh.

"There's something else," she said, before he could speak.

Andrews nodded, sipped his drink. "The CIA knows about us."

Pat's expression was unchanged, placid yet aware. "Are you surprised?"

"Not really," Andrews said. "And I don't think it matters."

"I'm glad they do know," Pat said. "It bolsters my confidence in them."

Andrews smiled and tossed down almost all of his drink, not because he craved it, but because suddenly he wanted to get back to bed and sleep. The high tension of the last week had broken down to a relieved weariness. His arms and legs were weighted.

He checked the lock on the door, turned off the TV and got beneath the covers beside Pat. He knew she would sleep the rest of the night nude, as she always did after they'd made love. In the morning, perhaps they'd make love again. Or simply lie talking and watch the day brighten on the other side of the closed drapes. Right now, Andrews looked forward to one possibility as much as the other. Maybe Pat was wrong about his libido.

Within less than a minute, Andrews felt himself dropping into the soft, secure blackness of sleep.

Pat Colombo lay with her head resting in the crook of his arm, not remembering the blond man in the supermarket.

In the morning they bought groceries at a store in the old shopping area of Perith, and they rented ski equipment at one of the new sports shops in the strip shopping center farther down the street.

They set off up the mountain, taking both cars so Pat could leave alone if it was decided that Andrews should stay longer. Andrews let Pat drive ahead of him up the treacherous winding road. If her low-slung sports car became stuck on a steep grade, he could easily prod it along with the powerful four-wheel-drive Jeep.

But the road was clear and dry until they'd driven high enough to be into snow. Pat's car negotiated the upper road with surprisingly little difficulty and had to be rescued by Andrews only once.

When at last they reached the cabin, snow was falling in fine, brittle flakes that were almost small hail pellets. Andrews carried in the groceries while Pat got the skis down from the Jeep's top carrier.

The cabin was small, but modern and conveniently appointed. On one wall of the main room was a huge stone fireplace flanked by well-stocked bookshelves. Off the other side of the room, beyond a grouping of a black-leather sofa and two matching chairs, was a small but complete kitchen equipped with a freezer and a microwave oven. In the loft above the main room were two small bedrooms, each with a double bed. If more heat was desired than was furnished by the oversized fireplace, a propane gas heater was concealed in the wall between kitchen and main room. On a table near the sofa was a telephone, but Andrews couldn't remember it ever ringing.

He checked the supply of firewood on the front porch and found it dry and plentiful. While Pat put away the groceries, Andrews built a loudly crackling fire in the stone fireplace. Within an hour the cabin was comfortably warm.

The rest of that day they read, skied, ate, made love. Felt safe.

29

Robert Arlen walked along Fifth Avenue to West Forty-second Street, down West Forty-second toward Broadway. He strolled casually through the cold, neon-glazed night as if he had no destination, seemingly preoccupied and unaware. But he was aware of everything going on around him.

Dressed in Andrews' dark slacks, black turtleneck sweater and tan jacket, the outfit he and Graham had decided was most distinctly Andrews' during his New York misadventures, Arlen stayed merely on the fringes of the areas that had been frequented by Andrews. From a distance, and not a very great distance, he would certainly be mistaken for Andrews. The same clothes, same mannerisms, same walk, same haunts.

Behind Arlen was another CIA agent, unobtrusive and watching. Ahead of Arlen was the trailing agent's counterpart. Both men were experts in the art of being invisible. So shadowed, Arlen felt as safe as possible under the circumstances. He was himself thoroughly trained in the martial arts, and he carried tucked in a leather holster in the small of his back a snubnosed Smith and Wesson .38 revolver that was an effective killer at close quarters. He had used it before and was confident of its deadliness.

Arlen had been walking for more than two hours now, and nothing suspicious had occurred. The bait remained untouched.

He was startled for a moment by a blast of sound, but it turned out to be only a slim black youth lugging one of those oversized tape players. The youth walked on at a purposeful fast clip, white vinyl boots flashing. The raucous music was soon lost in the mingled night sounds of Times Square.

After another hour on sidewalks now packed with tourists and theatergoers, Arlen decided that the night had been wasted. Stepping out of the way of a wizened gray-haired woman attentively being escorted by a swarthy young professional in a blue tuxedo, he headed back toward the Hayes Hotel.

He nodded to the old bellhop near the brass revolving door at the hotel entrance and crossed the carpeted lobby to the elevators. There was one other passenger in the elevator, a man carrying a salesman's sample case, a raincoat draped over his free arm. Arlen leaned against the steel wall of the elevator and nonchalantly moved his right hand around nearer his gun.

But the salesman, in the manner of elevator passengers, studiously avoided Arlen and surveyed the ceiling. At the third floor he got out and disappeared down the hall, walking as if he had sore feet, fishing in his pocket for his room key.

When he reached Andrews' room, Arlen flashed his ultraviolet penlight at the doorknob and saw that the chemical that glowed only under the flashlight beam was undisturbed. He unlocked the door and entered.

The room was silent, still lighted softly by the fixture in the alcove by the bathroom. Arlen took off his jacket and tossed it over a chair. Then he decided to remove the sweater. He hated turtlenecks. They were too confining. He didn't even like to wear a necktie.

As he crossed his arms and was pulling the sweater over his head, he heard the closet door open.

He managed to work one arm free before something was clamped firmly about his neck, cutting off his wind. Arlen didn't panic; he remembered that the room had been wired for sound and tried desperately to yell. But the pressure on his windpipe increased brutally, choking off sound. His free arm was pinned tightly behind him, up between his shoulder blades. Frantically, he thrashed out with his legs, trying to upset something to make enough noise to attract help. But the only sound was that of his feet thumping softly on the carpet.

The light behind his eyelids became red, deepened to a black that was dotted by bursting pinpoints of brightness. Then he was unfeeling, drifting . . .

"It shouldn't have happened," Underwood said.

Graham stood behind him, staring down at Arlen. "I don't understand how it could have."

Arlen was sitting on the sofa, rubbing his bruised and reddened neck. He said nothing; it hurt him almost unbearably to speak. When he had regained consciousness, he'd crawled slowly across the carpet in agony and deliberately knocked over a lamp, and within seconds the help that should have arrived an hour before burst in.

Graham was there almost immediately, and, shortly thereafter, Underwood. Underwood wore the annoyed, impatient look of a man who'd been bested at some highly competitive game because he'd allowed himself to become distracted.

With great pain and effort, Arlen explained to them what had happened.

Graham paced to the window. It was unlocked. "He might have lowered himself from one of the floors above," he said. "But dammit, Keeler across the street should have seen him!"

"Yet it *is* possible that he got in that way," Underwood said thoughtfully.

"It's the only way he could have got in, and he had to be lucky to get in that way."

"Or skillful," Underwood remarked. "Incredibly skillful."

"The rest was easy enough," Graham said. "Once he gained entry, he hid in the closet and waited for Andrews'— or Arlen's return. Then he chose his opportunity."

"And during the struggle, the sweater never was removed from around Arlen's head . . ."

Graham nodded. That was the one break they'd had, apparently. Aside from the fact that Arlen still was alive. "So even if our man would know the difference between the two men close up," Graham said, "he still thinks he killed Andrews."

Underwood walked to the window and looked outside. "But he didn't kill him. That's what worries me." He turned back toward Graham. "He was good enough to get in here without being seen, then he bungled the job. He didn't kill him."

"Then maybe he doesn't think he scored," Graham said. "Maybe he was scared off." He was watching Underwood carefully.

"It doesn't take long to garrote a man," Underwood said sharply. He sounded almost as if he were disappointed in the intruder for not completing his work. Graham, who knew Underwood as well as anyone did, realized that he was reacting to being puzzled. It disturbed Underwood to be puzzled.

Several people walked by outside in the hall, happily chattering about nothing consequential. A woman giggled. Theirs was a different world, with problems unlike those confronting the three men insulated in the room.

"We have to find a way now to let him know he failed in his attempt to kill Andrews," Graham said.

Underwood smiled, as if experiencing a sudden, subtle revelation. "Do we?" he said.

30

They liked to ski in the early-morning light, when the snow had a brittle white freshness about it and the pines and rocky crags cast distorting shadows that were dangerous. Andrews and Pat were both good skiers, though Andrews had taken up skiing only two years ago. Pat had skied since her college days in upper New York state.

For over an hour they tested their abilities on the angled slopes, sideslipping and doing difficult stem turns, building speed and feeling the freedom that skiing provides. As they swept across white spaces, Andrews admired the superior ability of the graceful figure in red jacket and stretch pants skiing ahead of him.

It was just cool enough to see faint wisps of vapor from their breathing as Andrews and Pat crouched low and traced a lazy, zigzag course back toward the cabin.

One of Andrews' boots came loose from its binding, and he flexed his knees and swiveled his hips, turning to brake with the edge of one long, sideways-flung ski. A spray of snow described a graceful pure arc as he stopped midway down the slope.

He watched Pat plant a ski pole, crouch lower and snake around a dark outcropping of rock as if it were a slalom pylon, as she continued toward the cabin.

Andrews knelt and carefully refastened the boot in its binding. In the silence of the mountain he could hear the soft rasping of his breathing, and cold began seeping along his flesh where his gloves didn't quite meet his jacket sleeves and the back of his shirt had stretched and risen above his belt.

By the time he'd straightened and was ready to continue down the slope, Pat had disappeared beyond the stand of pines near the cabin. Andrews reflected that she probably was already leaning her skis against the wall by the door, or possibly was already inside, sitting on the sofa removing her ski boots and heavy wool socks. He leaned forward, planted his ski poles and pushed off down the mountain.

He hadn't gone far when he saw a dark rise of rock slightly to the left of his projected path.

Alarms jangled in the back of his mind. Andrews had skied for two seasons on the mountain, and he didn't remember that angle of rock emerging above snow this deep. He began to snowplow to slow his speed as he approached the dark protruberance.

From a hundred feet away, he saw that it was not a rock; its contour was too smooth and strangely symmetrical.

From fifty feet away, he saw that what he'd mistaken for a rock was a body, lying facedown, partly on its side and half concealed by the light snow that had fallen last night. A sudden breeze momentarily covered the dark form with a powdery white shroud.

Andrews spun to the side, digging in his poles, and stood staring down at the body.

It was the corpse of a man, hatless, dressed in a twisted blue overcoat pulled halfway up over the back of his head. The face wasn't visible.

Andrews felt his numbness wear off to be replaced by confusion, an enraged sort of pity for the man at his feet and then fear. He made himself kneel and clutch the stiff material of the coat. Then he forced himself to shift the body so he could see the face.

He stood up with a hollow, inward breath of shock.

The dead man was Underwood. He'd been strangled by a thin wire with such force that his throat had been cut to create beneath his chin a gaping, lipless red grin.

"Fall down, slowpoke?" Pat asked Andrews from where she sat curled in a corner of the sofa. The fire Andrews had laid before they left the cabin was now crackling and blazing, shadowing Pat's face in subtle mobile tones and brightening her eyes.

Andrews locked the cabin door behind him. He'd left his skis on the porch.

Gravity seemed to increase and overcome the contented expression on Pat Colombo's face. "What's wrong?" she asked, in a voice also slowed by ponderous weight.

"I found a body up the slope."

Pat didn't understand what he meant.

"A dead body," Andrews said. "It's Samuel Underwood."

For several seconds Pat stared at him. "The same Underwood . . . ?" She knew her question was unnecessary and let her voice trail off.

"The same," Andrews said. He was unexpectedly calm, yet his heart was racing. The sudden heat of the cabin was beginning to make him perspire.

"What does it mean?" Pat asked. "What was he doing here?"

Andrews crossed the room, removed his down ski jacket and tried to think of the answers to Pat's questions. He could think of nothing but the horror-struck, puzzled expression on Underwood's face, and the unnatural gaping grin beneath his chin. *What did it mean?* he repeated Pat's question to himself. *Could any of it be explained?*

The telephone rang.

Andrews' body jerked as if the sound had penetrated his flesh.

No one could know they were here. And the telephone had ceased to exist to Andrews; it had never rung. Never.

It rang two more times while he stood frozen. It was the only sound in the world.

He walked to the phone, and on the fifth ring he lifted the receiver and raised it to his ear.

"Senator Andrews," a deep, level voice said, "this is Paul Liggett."

31

Nels Graham's car was in the lead as the three identical late-model gray Pontiacs threaded their way up the narrow highway toward the isolated town of Perith. They were now the only cars on that remote section of highway, traveling above the posted cautionary speed limit, maintaining equal distances from each other, conveying a sense of perfectly controlled haste.

Graham sat next to his driver, Tom Mathison, peering through the windshield at the increasingly steep and rocky country around them. To his left and higher, he could see vast fields of white through slowly dissipating mist, and here and there off the sides of the highway were isolated, irregular patches of snow preserved in low spots. Graham turned his head slightly sideways and forward to squint up at the sky. There was plenty of blue showing, but a bank of low gray clouds appeared to be moving in, devouring the blue in a measured and unstoppable advance.

He was watching a spidery, windblown pattern of light snow cross the highway when the car suddenly braked to a halt, sharply enough to pitch him forward so that he had to support himself with a hand on the padded dashboard.

"Jesus!" he said, glancing at Mathison.

Mathison merely nodded, a single forward pecking motion,

indicating that Graham should look in the direction they had been driving.

On the crest of a slight rise in the highway, where the mountain sloped down on the left and there was a steep drop to the right, a rockslide had blocked the road.

"Isn't that just fine!" Graham said with acid irony.

He and Mathison got out of the warm car and walked forward to examine the rockslide more closely. Two men from the other cars joined them. They all stood for a few seconds without speaking, soberly confronting the unexpected obstacle.

The rockslide was over five feet high and extended the width of the road. Some of the smaller rocks had gone over the edge of the highway to scatter on the slope beyond. There was no way to clear a path for the cars, no way to go around the blockage.

"How far is Perith?" Graham asked Mathison. He was shivering. It was cold at this altitude.

"About five miles."

Graham stared thoughtfully out over the sweep of angled, pine-covered mountainside. A hawk, or possibly a small vulture, circled effortlessly with fixed wings against a blue patch of morning sky, as if flaunting its freedom.

"Let's look at the map," Graham said, "and see if there's a way around this mess."

He returned with Mathison to the car and they spread the road map out on the hood. The turned-off engine began to tick rapidly. Metal cooling.

"This way looks best," Mathison suggested after a few minutes. He traced a squarish forefinger along the crinkled map.

Graham followed the course of the fingertip with his eyes. The heat rising from the car's hood felt good in the brisk air. "That means going all the way back to the main highway," he said, when Mathison was finished.

"But it looks like the surest way, sir."

Graham bent closer to study the map. "This way would be shorter." His own forefinger traced a course.

"That doesn't look like much of a road," Mathison said, pointing to the faint blue line that cut from highway to highway. "And it might be closed off just like this one."

"It's worth the chance," Graham said. "It saves miles." He glanced quickly about. "Can we turn the cars around here?" he asked, with sudden doubt that wasn't revealed in his voice.

"Sure," Mathison said, "but it'll be touchy."

Graham nodded. "Let's tell the others what's going on."

"Yes, sir." Mathison reached through the rolled-down window and tapped the horn.

"Not that way!" Graham snapped, shooting an upward glance at the looming mountain that had produced the rockslide. "You'll kill us all."

32

Andrews' hand was pale and tight around the telephone receiver. The inside of the cabin seemed to become smaller, to lurch in time and space. A voice that Andrews recognized as his own asked, "Who are you?"

"I told you," the calm and chilling answering voice on the phone said, "Paul Liggett. I saw you find Samuel Underwood's body on the slope, Senator."

"Karpp!"

"Liggett," the voice corrected.

Andrews refused to make that small concession to insanity. "Whoever you are, what do you want?"

"You, Senator. I want you. And your lady."

Andrews' initial shock and fear had dulled somewhat, lodged like something heavy and solid within him. There was room now for anger, for the will to survive a situation he had sensed the moment he'd seen Underwood dead. "Did you kill Underwood?" It was a needless question, but Andrews felt he needed a spoken confirmation to underpin his own determination that he and Pat should live.

"Of course I did. Killing is why I'm here. It's why I exist."

Andrews was watching Pat Colombo stare at him. Her body was tense beneath bulky gray sweater and red stretch pants, her face lined with concern and puzzlement. Andrews wondered what she must see on his own face.

"Why did you kill him?" he asked the voice that claimed to be Paul Liggett's. He saw fear replace puzzlement on Pat's normally placid features.

"It was Underwood who killed himself, in a way," the voice said. "I was only the instrument of his destruction, while he was the instigator. He moved of his own volition toward oblivion. As you have done, Senator. You have carried death with you for some time now, and you've brought it here with you to this cabin. Of course, you'll be required to share it with Miss Colombo. Will she mind?"

"Listen, you maniac—"

"Oh, I wouldn't say I'm a maniac," the voice interrupted. "I might more accurately be described as an extension of a maniac's inspired mind—yes, I think you could call me that."

"Do you seriously expect me to believe you're Paul Liggett?"

"But you do believe it, Senator. That's why I'm here."

And with a cold rush of revelation, Andrews knew that at least a part of his mind did believe. It wasn't the logical center of his mind, it was the instinctual fringe. The primal. That really was what frightened him.

"There are many things we might talk about, Senator," Ligget said, "but I'm afraid there'll be no more such communication between you and me. Between you and anyone. You're dead, Senator."

Andrews heard the click and buzz of the broken connection. Then, abruptly, even the buzz was gone. The phone wire leading from the cabin had been cut.

He stood for a while holding the silent receiver pressed painfully to his ear. The pain at least was real, at the moment the only thing certifiably real in Andrews' world. He knew he had to shake that dreamlike sensation of helplessness. Slowly he replaced the dead receiver.

"Jerry?" It was Pat's voice. "What's going on? Who was that you were talking to?"

/ 177

Andrews looked at her, drew comfort from the sight despite her obvious fear. Her fright was a reflection of his own, he realized, and he tried to remove from his face all indication of the terror that prowled his mind.

"It was Martin Karpp," he said. "Or Paul Liggett, as he called himself."

Pat's right hand lightly traced the coarse material of her bulky sweater. "Karpp's locked in a sanitarium over a thousand miles from here," she said.

"Yes."

"So explain."

"I can't. And he wouldn't." Andrews sounded incongruously flip.

Pat walked to one of the chairs before the blaze in the fireplace and sat down. She seemed now to possess more calm than fear, but Andrews knew that her fear had rooted and was now as constant as it was invisible.

"Why did he phone?" she asked. "Was it about Underwood?"

"About Underwood," Andrews said. "And about us."

Her dark eyes seemed to deepen as she nodded. "I see. Now he has to kill us. But wouldn't it have been smarter not to phone, to surprise us instead?"

"He saw me find Underwood's body," Andrews said. He walked nearer to the fire and leaned into the radiating heat. "He knows that we know. And he phoned for another reason. He, it—whatever we're dealing with—knows about paralyzing with fear."

A crescent of smooth muscle flexed along Pat's jaw. "Then forget about that 'it' and 'whatever' part. There's a man out there, not some murderous walking figment of somebody's imagination."

"If there really was someone on the other end of the phone," Andrews said. "If the voice wasn't a figment of *my* imagination."

For an instant Pat's eyes were shot with fear again. "Don't talk like that, Jerry! I heard the phone ring." She jerked her head to stare at the phone. "Why don't we call for help?"

"He must have tapped a portable unit into the phone line near the cabin to make his call, then he cut the wire."

"Then it wasn't your imagination that did *that*," Pat said. "Or are you going to suggest there's some sort of doppelganger out there created by your own fear?"

"It had occurred to me," Andrews admitted. He saw that he was frightening Pat deeply with his admitted irrationality. "We have to put aside all suppositions of the supernatural if we're going to get out of here," he said, and she seemed relieved. She saw the Andrews she knew.

Andrews found himself wondering just how solid a figment of the imagination could become, and, following his own advice, he thrust the thought away. He walked toward the door.

"Where are you going?" Pat asked in alarm.

"Nowhere, I'm sure."

Carefully, gradually, Andrews edged open the door.

A bullet smacked into the doorframe inches from his head. As he hurled himself backward something stung the right side of his face, very near his eye.

He was sitting on the floor, staring at the door that he'd instinctively closed. Fueled by fear, his heart was on a rampage. The reverberations of Pat's scream still played in the air.

Andrews stood up on unsteady legs, planted his feet.

"You're bleeding," Pat said in a hoarse, somehow sensuous voice.

He stood bent over while she removed a long splinter of wood from the flesh beneath his right cheekbone and showed it to him.

The shot had come from higher on the mountain, and it had been fired to kill. A man with a rifle, Andrews thought; that was unmistakably real. He raised his hand and wiped away traces of blood from his cheek. He was lucky one of the wood splinters hadn't lodged in his eye.

"Are there any firearms in the cabin?" Pat asked.

"None." Andrews looked at her. His anger and fear were cold things now, held below the necessity for action. He smiled and kissed her on the forehead. Her flesh was cool and dry. "We'll figure some way out," he told her.

Pat returned the smile, said nothing. She was more afraid of this sudden deadly reality than of the threat of the unreal. She knew little about Martin Karpp.

Walking slowly about the cabin, carefully peering from each curtained window, Andrews attempted to assess their situation. Except for the cleared area in front of the cabin, crisp accumulated snow nearly a foot deep covered the ground. On two sides of the cabin sparse woods stretched away on the mountain face, thickening rapidly as the ground descended beyond the timberline. Most of the mountain above the cabin was blanketed by the unbroken snow, but there was plenty of room for concealment provided by slope configuration and occasional jutting rocks or shrouded tree stumps. From above, both the rear and front doors of the cabin were visible and afforded clear shots. And, except for the small kitchen window, the cabin's only windows faced front and rear. But exit from the kitchen window would be concealed by the cabin's walls for only a few feet, then anyone on that side of the cabin would also be within range of rifle fire from above.

Andrews' rented four-wheel-drive Jeep was parked about fifty feet from the front door, its blunt nose aimed up the mountain. Pat's red sports car was parked nearer, but farther around toward the side of the cabin. It, too, was facing the wrong way for a fast escape.

Surprising their assailant and skiing quickly out of range down mountain seemed a slim possibility, only both Andrews' and Pat's skis were propped against the wall outside on the cabin's small porch. Even if they survived bringing the skis inside, the act would tip their plan.

Andrews turned to face the center of the cabin, the point beyond which fear multiplied in every direction. As his mind traced the perimeter of their predicament, desperately seeking some way out, hopelessness seeped into him, crumbling his will. He was a junkie hooked on dread. Again he told himself that was why who or whatever was out there had phoned, to unnerve them and to bring about that curious inertia of deep terror. But he couldn't control his reaction to that strategy.

The cabin itself actually provided little refuge. The armed stalker could enter virtually at will and slay the weaponless Andrews and Pat. Or the cabin could be riddled with bullets from the outside. Perhaps even put to the torch to drive its doomed occupants into the open. The killing ground. The assault could occur at any moment, and it certainly would take place before dark.

You're dead, Senator.

Paul Liggett had told him that as if stating a simple fact.

Pat was seated with her hands folded pale and limp in her lap, like stricken creatures that were separate from her. She was staring up at Andrews, her protector, waiting for him to explain to her how they might survive.

Andrews had nothing to tell her.

33

It had begun to snow large flakes so laden with moisture that they were barely affected by the breeze and dropped almost straight down. The narrow roads leading to the small self-sufficient town of Perith were becoming more hazardous by the minute, and visibility was decreasing.

Graham and Mathison, in the lead car of the three agency sedans bound for Perith, sat in silence, watching the deteriorating weather conditions. Mathison was driving, hunched forward over the wheel and squinting out through the windshield while he skillfully applied brake and accelerator to hold the big Pontiac on the unpredictable road. To the left of the cars was steep mountain, and to the right steep drop.

"This is the shittiest country to drive in I've ever seen," Mathison said suddenly. It was uncharacteristic of him to curse. He used the cuff of his coat to wipe away some of the mist that persistently formed on the inside of the windshield. The defroster wasn't working right.

"We'll get where we're trying to go," Graham said, though he was beginning to doubt it. He glanced at Mathison from the corner of his eye, saw no change of expression on the agent's impassive features. Graham knew that Mathison was sitting there being glad that following this route to Perith hadn't been his decision.

Graham turned to look out the side window at the silent

maelstrom of snow, consoling himself with the thought that there was no way he could have predicted the weather. There were times in the past few days, and especially today, when he felt that he was involved in one of those desperate situations in which fate had decreed that he should fail. The windshield wipers began to screech on the cold glass, torturing Graham's taut nerves, as if sensing his vulnerability.

He strained to see ahead, his imagination filling in the blurred outline of a white mound that appeared to block the road.

But before Graham could say anything to Mathison, he saw that the road swung right and flanked the irregularity in the mountainside. For a moment Graham had thought they'd come up against another rockslide. That would have finished them in their efforts to reach Perith. That would have finished a lot of things.

The wipers emitted a particularly loud and grating squeal.

"Can you turn those goddamn things on low?" Graham asked.

Mathison gave him a quick sideways glance, more with the head than the eyes. "I can't see very far past the end of the hood now, sir."

Graham knew Mathison was right, that he, Graham, had let nerves override logic. The wipers would squeal and that was that. "Okay. If it makes that much difference—"

Graham's words were chopped off as his mouth snapped shut, and his heart seemed to expand as the car suddenly lurched to the right and downward. He heard Mathison's sharp gasp, was aware of Mathison's right foot frantically jerking from accelerator to brake.

For a dizzying instant Graham thought that the car might move again, lurch one more time into the terrifying smoothness of space. But it didn't.

After a few seconds, Graham allowed himself to believe that it wouldn't.

The engine had died and they were still. Mathison sat stiffly in the driver's seat. His foot had slipped from the brake pedal and his gloved hands were trembling on the steering wheel.

"We're both going to get out slowly," Graham told him, "on your side. Open the door."

But there was no need for Mathison to open the door. One of the agents from the following car already was easing it open.

"I think the car'll hold," he was saying, "but move slow and careful. The front wheel's over."

"The emergency brake wouldn't be a bad idea," Graham said. Mathison nodded and smoothly but firmly depressed the pedal with his left foot.

Graham waited, not moving, while Mathison inched cautiously toward the door on the driver's side. Mathison seemed almost to be levitating by sheer will, only now and then barely touching the seat beneath him.

When Mathison was all the way out, and the car hadn't budged, Graham began to slide across the incline of the seat to the open door, holding his breath. His instincts screamed at him that any second the car was going to roll into nothingness.

As he drew in his stomach to pass beneath the steering wheel, hands clutched his arm and helped him. Strong fingers dug deeply and painfully into his bicep.

On unsteady legs, he found himself standing on the icy road outside the car. It was a pleasure the way the ground seemed to press up against the soles of his shoes.

After a few minutes, Graham and the three agents examined the car. It was nose down over the side of the road, the right front wheel dangling. Though it had been impossible to tell from inside, the car had really been in no great danger of going all the way over the edge. Yet there was no way, other than the use of a tow truck, to haul it back away from the precipice. Having ventured one cautious wheel into space, it seemed to cling petrified to its present security. It blocked the road.

"There's no way around it," Mathison said. "We're done."

Graham stood feeling the sting of cold snowflakes on his face. One of them landed on his eyelash and melted, momentarily blurring his vision. He again had the sensation that some malicious spirit was deliberately creating obstacles in his path.

It seemed suddenly very cold. Graham thrust his fists deep in his topcoat pockets and walked to the edge of the road, standing near the rear of the car and peering down into the whirling white void.

"There's a way past," he said. "We push the car the rest of the way over."

Mathison stood with his mouth open, his bureaucratic mind aghast. One simply didn't so blatantly destroy agency property. The other agents stood with blank, unquestioning faces. This was a need-to-know operation. Only Graham was fully aware of the desperate situation they were in. Even now, he wasn't inclined to share part of that information. He had his own plans. He always had his own plans. That was what made him different from Mathison, what guaranteed his future.

"Release the emergency brake," Graham instructed Mathison. "We'll clear the road and proceed in two cars."

Brushing snow from his eyebrows with his gloved hand, Mathison turned and obeyed.

The four men got behind the car and pushed in unison. Ice and rock scraped softly, then loudly, against the car's underside as its balance shifted. Rending metal screamed as if protesting the atrocity that was happening.

The rear wheels suddenly were off the ground, the chrome bumper smoothly rising and falling away from the agents' hands. With somehow awesome abruptness, the car was gone.

After an unnervingly long time, the eerie sound of its impact on the mountainside rose to them through the cold air, muffled by the snow.

The weather was clear in Manhattan. Amos Franks was driving his department car on Sixth Avenue, past Rockefeller Center, when he heard the radio request for Homicide. The address was on East Fifty-fourth Street, not far from where he was right now. He cranked down the windows, fastened the cherry light to the outside of the roof and accelerated across an intersection against a light that had just changed to red. A mass of pedestrians standing at the curb waiting to cross glared at him, and in one of the irregular intermittent instants of silence in the siren's warbling wail he heard someone shout angrily at him.

The East Fifty-fourth Street address turned out to belong to something called Bargain Electronics. Franks pulled his car to the curb behind an angled-in police cruiser. A large uniformed cop was at the door of the electronics shop, standing staunchly with hands on hips. Franks got out, ambled around the car and toward the cop. When he got close enough, he flashed his shield in case the cop wouldn't recognize him.

"Straight on in, Captain," the cop said.

A crowd had gathered outside. As Franks shoved open the door to the shop, he heard the stalwart cop order everyone to move along, relishing his lines.

The inside of Bargain Electronics was cluttered with displays of cameras, recorders, radios and stereo equipment. Two detectives from Homicide were standing with another uniformed patrolman near a pyramid of boxes containing portable radios shaped like popular soft drink bottles.

One of the detectives, a tall, jowly man Franks remembered as Benny or Barney, recognized Franks and shot him a grave glance. "Right here, sir," he said, motioning down toward the floor with his head. Franks saw a foot protruding from behind the base of the pyramid of radios. It was clad in one of those crinkly-leather Italian loafers with built-up heels.

"Everyone's on the way," the other detective said, meaning the M.E., fingerprint crew and a police photographer.

Franks stepped behind the display and felt his stomach do a loop as he looked down at the man on the floor. He was a short, overweight man, middle-aged, with graying hair and classic features that suggested a long ago Spain far removed from Manhattan's East Side. And he was as dead as any of those long-ago Spaniards. He was lying very gracefully on his back with his arms flung over his head. On his shirt front was a scarlet bib of congealed blood. A thin wire was around his neck, and it had cut his throat as savagely and deeply as Franks had ever seen a throat cut. There was, Franks thought, an almost inhuman callous efficiency to this method of killing.

"How long's he been dead?" he asked the detectives.

"We'll have to let the M.E. tell us," the jowly one, whose name Franks suddenly remembered was Bernie Addles, replied. "The store was closed today. The kid who helps out here came in about half an hour ago to do some inventory work and stumbled across the body."

"He the one who called us?"

Addles nodded. "He's sitting down in the room in back. Want to talk to him?"

"Later," Franks said. He glanced around at the displays of expensive electronic products, some of the most popular merchandise of thieves. "Robbery?" he asked.

Bernie Addles shrugged his slumped shoulders. "As of now, it appears that nothing was taken." Addles held up a black trifold wallet he'd removed from the dead man. "His name was Vincent Grammo, fifty-three years old, lived out in Queens." Addles lowered the wallet. The wrinkled green corner of a bill was sticking out of it. "There's over a hundred bucks in here," Addles said. "So far we haven't found the weapon . . ."

Suddenly Franks was barely listening. It had taken him a few beats to remember where he'd heard the name Vincent Grammo, the name of the dead man in the Italian loafers.

There was a commotion toward the front of the store as two fingerprint men came in accompanied by an assistant to the medical examiner.

"So where's the object of all this attention?" the assistant M.E. inquired, with what seemed to be genuine morbid cheer.

Franks got out of his way, stepped back from the knot of softly conversing men near the body. He nodded to Bernie Addles, then turned and left Bargain Electronics. The police photographer arrived just in time to pull into Franks' vacated parking space behind the cruiser.

In his office, Franks sat down behind his desk and thought about Senator Jerry Andrews sitting across from him and mentioning Vincent Grammo's name along with the names of two other people who had since died violent deaths. He thought of Vincent Grammo, sprawled with freeze-frame elegance on the floor of his electronics store with his throat gaping.

With a glance to make sure his office door was closed, Franks reached into a bottom desk drawer and withdrew a bottle of scotch and a clear plastic cup. He poured himself a drink.

And then another.

34

Andrews gazed out the cabin window at a sharp protective angle, watching the moisture-laden snow fall to form a slick and glistening patina over the snow already on the ground. An idea had worked its way into his mind. A dangerous idea. At first he had rejected it as suicidal—and maybe it was. Then the snow had begun to fall, impairing visibility just enough so that Andrews and Pat might have a chance, and the idea became a plan.

If they were going to take advantage of the snow, Andrews decided, it should be soon. Then he wondered, would whoever was out there, calculating to kill, anticipate that the snowfall might prompt Andrews to act? If so, the odds on Andrews and Pat escaping were reduced even further, bordering on the unacceptable.

Andrews shook himself out of that rut of pessimism. The snow was a break. It provided Andrews and Pat with an opportunity that the stalker couldn't have foreseen. They would be foolish not to attempt to use what little leverage they'd lucked into. Andrews turned to face Pat, who was still seated in the flickering reflection from the fireplace.

"Give me your car keys," he told her. "Then I'm going to explain something to you."

She seemed to come alert, as if suddenly reassured that Andrews was again in firm command of the situation. His request for the keys must mean that he'd figured out some way for them to leave, and she trusted him. He hoped she'd continue to trust him after hearing what he proposed.

When Andrews was finished talking, he watched Pat's face but could see nothing of her reaction. She sat silently for a long time, her thoughts private as she pondered the likelihood of imminent death.

"It will get us killed or save us," she said, in a voice both somber and dignified.

"At least we're exercising an option," Andrews told her. "Not simply sitting here on the defensive." He made himself stop talking. He had laid out the plan for Pat to accept or reject; he didn't want to sell her on it. He didn't feel that strongly about their chances himself.

"We should try it," she said at last. She gave Andrews an incredible smile that belied the circumstances. "I've heard for years about the element of surprise. If this works, everyone else will hear about it for years."

And if it doesn't work . . . Andrews thought. But their decision had been reached. He refused even to consider the possibility of failure. Not now. There existed only two alternatives for them, and only one of those alternatives meant life.

They put on coats and boots, and then stood in silence. Only the soft, whispering patter of the falling snow, somehow urgent, penetrated the vacuum of the ominous lull.

Andrews looked at Pat. She seemed incapable of the needed speed and motion in her bulky down jacket. But Andrews knew that he appeared the same way. Ski clothing was deceptive. It was actually light and afforded plenty of freedom of movement. Pat adjusted her red and black stocking cap and nodded to Andrews.

He picked up the remote-control starter switch for the rented Jeep and walked to the kitchen window. They would gain a few steps by leaving through this window. Pat touched

Andrews' right arm. He could hear her breathing rapidly, unevenly, as slowly and quietly he raised the window in its weather-warped frame.

Surprisingly cold air carried a mild flurry of large snowflakes into the cabin. Andrews felt a few of the flakes on his face, grateful for them, and watched several large white flecks appear on his silky blue jacket sleeve and begin to melt. At least the snow hadn't let up, but the visibility outside wasn't as poor as it had seemed through the closed window.

For a second Andrews wondered if he would have the courage demanded by his own plan. There was, of course, only one way to know for sure. Determination, enthusiasm, patriotic and bracing euphemisms—under real, underwear-fouling duress, all of that disappeared like smoke in the wind, and courage became a thing in the very pit of the soul that either you were born with or you were not. Andrews would soon know his inheritance.

With exaggerated, slow movements, he climbed out through the open window, keeping his body tight against the outside of the cabin. He was clutching the remote-control switch in his bare right hand. The Jeep was to his right, about fifty feet away. Pat's red sports car was parked nearer by about ten feet, its windshield coated with unmarked snow. Like the Jeep, it gave the impression that it was rooted to the icy terrain, impossible to coax into mechanical life and motion.

Andrews swiveled his body, extended an arm to help Pat out the window. The thought flashed through his mind that this was like a grotesque elopement, and all those people who in jokes compared weddings to funerals might know what they were talking about. He caught a glimpse of Pat's pasty, rigid features framing determined eyes. A large snowflake settled on one of her dark lashes as he spoke to her.

"Be ready," he said, the words ripping hoarse and fierce from his throat. Her face softened for a moment, then regained its solemn stiffness as she nodded. Andrews pressed the remote-control button to turn over the Jeep's engine fifty feet away.

At first nothing happened, and despite his fear Andrews actually felt an acute embarrassment. He stared in perplexity at the Jeep through the white dance of the snow, frustrated by its betrayal.

The Jeep's starter groaned, softly at first, then very loud, like a thing in agony. The engine coughed twice but didn't catch.

A shot cracked the brittle mountain air and echoed in diminishing reverberations.

But Andrews and Pat were already running, not toward the Jeep but toward the sports car. Andrews continued to keep his thumb jammed on the remote starter button.

He was aware of the Jeep's windows exploding in a shower of snow and bits of safety glass as shot after shot rolled in a continual volley along snow-crusted slopes. And he knew suddenly that there was more than one rifle firing and felt a numbing stab of fear. If he'd been wrong about *that*! . . .

Pat was running beside him, keeping up. Her leg brushed his. Their booted ankles crossed, became momentarily tangled, and they almost fell. But they kept their footing and threw themselves gasping into the sports car.

The shooting had stopped. As Andrews fumbled to insert the key in the ignition switch, he knew why. Surprise no longer applied. The gunmen had realized that the Jeep was empty and were shifting their aim to the sports car.

The cold metal about the keyhole deflected the key. Andrews dropped it, caught it.

Miraculously, it slipped into its slot easily on the next try. After two quick turnovers, the car's engine snarled to eager life.

Pat reached over and flipped the wiper switch so Andrews could see as the car reversed, then skidded in a wild U-turn and headed for the road. Andrews hadn't been aware of more shots, but he saw snow flick off the center of the hood and heard the blunt hammer blow of metal penetrating metal. As he wrenched the wheel to the left, feeling the car lose traction, then the gradual bite of the tires once more, something snapped loudly past his right ear and the windshield cracked into a star pattern before his startled eyes. Even as he was blindly taking the first turn down the harrowing slick mountain road, he was smashing out with his fist, feeling the rush of stinging cold air as the shards of glass fell away and he could see. Vaguely, he was aware that his hand was bleeding.

"Just drive!" Pat screamed in his ear, and she began to strike at the rest of the glass with her gloved fist, eyes squinted for protection against the snow and windshield splinters.

Andrews' heart seemed to stop as the car fishtailed and he saw only space and swirling snow. He played the wheel to the left and then the right with a skill that some detached part of his mind observed in surprise and admiration. He glanced at Pat. She seemed all right. He seemed all right. With a sudden elation Andrews believed they could make it. They *would* make it!

He tapped the small brake pedal in short butterfly strokes before the next icy turn, guided the car through with a new confidence and hope. Beside him Pat was laughing crazily, tearfully, in a wild release of tension.

The mountain leveled off somewhat and the road straightened. The land was flatter now, and there were fewer drops. Instead of curving about the mountain face like an abstract corkscrew, the narrow, slippery road ran a straighter though still difficult course toward the base of the mountain. They were below the timberline, and the sparse woods flashing past on the right were becoming denser as the car dropped lower toward the valley. The road was more manageable but still unpredictable, demanding as much driving skill as Andrews possessed. He built his speed on the straightaways and came to near-stops to slide around the hairpin curves.

Even the biting, snow-flecked wind in his face felt good to Andrews. It meant he was alive—would continue to live! He noticed a slender glass splinter protruding from the web of flesh between the thumb and forefinger of his right hand but didn't bother to remove it. It didn't hurt. The hand was numb from the rush of cold air.

Then Andrews became aware of Pat's hand clutching his shoulder with a desperate strength to gain his attention. Andrews turned his head briefly toward her. She pointed. And he saw.

Through the trees Andrews could make out a shadowy crouched figure, now visible in flashes, now gone, trailing the car like a ghost. A skier, plunging down the slope almost parallel to the road.

The slope described a straighter line to the base of the mountain than did the twisting road, enabling the swift and skillful skier to keep pace. Andrews knew that if the skier reached the base of the mountain before the car, he would have time to set up and be waiting with his rifle. They were in a race now, and Andrews had to win it.

His right foot went to the accelerator, and he held his left poised over the brake pedal to butterfly the brakes before curves. The low red car picked up speed, momentarily dropped a wheel off the road shoulder. The branches of a large fir tree slapped and scraped at the hood and fender as Andrews jerked the steering wheel to the left and headed them for the next icy dip and curve. Pat was sitting motionless beside him, her arms straight out in front of her, hands spread and braced against the dashboard. As Andrews skidded the car wide and turned to the right, he leaned in that direction as if his weight might influence centrifugal force. Breath and heartbeat returned as the car came out of the curve and sped downhill through the whirling maze of snowflakes. Andrews thought he caught a glimpse of the indistinct figure of the skier flashing smoothly alongside beyond the trees, back bent, head lowered and arms tucked in at the sides, ski poles horizontal and trailing like twin dark comet tails. Then another curve appeared ahead, rushed toward them, as Andrews hunched his body over the wheel and played brake and accelerator.

This time the car did leave the road. Branches ticked the metal fenders. Pat screamed and was tossed sideways into Andrews, for a second causing his hands to leave the wheel. In that instant the car began violently rocking. Snow from overhead branches cascaded down through the broken windshield like cold water dashed on Andrews and Pat. There was a jolt and a loud rending sound as the right fender scraped a large outcropping of black rock.

The car veered left but remained upright. Andrews suddenly realized inanely that neither he nor Pat had fastened their safety belts. Pat was slumped forward, her head between her knees, her hands laced in her dark hair beneath her knit stocking cap. As Andrews watched, the cap slipped from her head and dropped to the floor. The wind caught her hair.

Andrews' gaze flicked upward just in time to see an onrushing huge tree. He spun the steering wheel to the left in panic, losing traction. The tree flashed past inches from the car's right side, like a telephone pole glimpsed from a roaring train. Branches snagged on the rear bumper, ripping it off. Another branch tore away most of the canvas convertible top.

But it was the tree that saved them. The impact of its branches had slowed the small car just enough to enable Andrews to regain control. Back on the road, he tapped the brake lightly, gripped the steering wheel with white-knuckled hands and peered through the smashed windshield with eyes glazed by equal parts of fright and resolve. He was familiar with the terrain and knew they were more than halfway down the mountain.

A guarded quick look to the right informed Andrews that the shadowy pursuer was still with them, almost as if, as Pat had once denied, projected by their fear.

The road flattened out for a relatively long stretch after the next S-curve. Andrews could pull away from the skier there, even though the slope beyond the trees was clear and fast. He negotiated the tricky double curve almost automatically, bent forward over the steering wheel and mashed down with his right foot on the accelerator.

"He's falling back!" Pat shouted.

Darting a glance to his right, Andrews saw that the skier was gradually losing ground. Holding to the center of the road, he pushed the car faster, teeth chattering violently as the tires hammered over washboards of ice. He knew that ahead, on the final leg to the bottom of the mountain, the road again became snaking and treacherous. The slope at that point was wide and steep, the snow perfect for skiing.

With a dread that he refused to convey to Pat, Andrews realized that actually they were losing. The figure on skis would be able to overtake and then race ahead of the car there, and be waiting for them either at some spot along the road or at the base of the mountain. For a moment Andrews toyed with the idea of trying to turn the car around or delaying their descent, but he remembered that there was another rifleman behind them, possibly following. He kept the car at top speed. It was the only thing he could do.

His mind darted ahead, recalling every dip and turn in the road, already figuring out how to cope with them. His familiarity with the mountain face was his only weapon.

Then he remembered a stretch of road that curved sharply before the final run to the valley, and Andrews knew how to use that one weapon. The mountain face was irregular there, rising in long, tailing ripples of rock. And it was at the point where the road curved that a skier traversing the slope had to cross the road. Andrews' foot went to the brake, applied light pressure.

Pat felt the slackening in their speed and looked over at him with questioning dark eyes. He said nothing. Not wanting the brake lights to wink on—if they still worked—he slipped the car into a lower gear and slowed again almost imperceptibly. He wanted it to appear that he still was wringing every inch of speed possible from the car.

Now the skier was moving almost exactly paralled with them, only about a hundred yards behind. Andrews tried to keep him there and managed to do so without difficulty. It was as if car and skier existed in their own time frame, with each second slowed and prodigiously important. Andrews negotiated several curving drops in the road and the skier gained. That was all right. It was almost time.

The sharp curve was coming up, and the skier disappeared beyond thick trees and a snow-covered rise. Andrews hit the brakes hard, cutting the car's speed almost in half. He would need precise timing. The car went into the curve at thirty miles per hour. Andrews kept his foot on the brake but reduced pressure.

The skier appeared like a sorcerer's illusion, flashing around the snowy mound of rock. He still expected the car to be ahead of him; he had to be surprised.

Now Andrews hit the accelerator. There was no way for the skier to dig his ski edges in and stop. No opportunity to change direction. Andrews caught a vivid glimpse of a darkly clad figure wearing a ski mask and goggles, arms upraised in alarm, ski poles falling away. It struck the side of the moving car at full speed.

The jolt actually moved the car sideways. Something dark flew over the tattered convertible top. A ski was hurled into the air, spinning like a helicopter rotor. And then the car began to spin.

Andrews yanked on the steering wheel without the slightest effect. The world had become a whirling, snow-filled carnival ride, building to dizzying speed.

Then the ride stopped, though the world continued to rock gently.

Equilibrium returned to Andrews. Pat was sprawled against him, one arm through the spokes of the steering wheel, shaking her head as if trying to clear her mind. There was a cut in the center of her forehead, but it wasn't bleeding badly.

Andrews saw that the car was wedged between two towering fir trees, tilted at an angle extreme enough to keep the now struggling Pat pressed to him. A noise to his right and behind him made Andrews swivel his head painfully. He saw a car.

It was useless even to try to scramble out of the crazily canted sports car. The car behind him, a large dark sedan, already had stopped and its doors were opening. Beside him, Pat sighed softly. Neither of them knew what to expect. They had done their best and were finished.

A dark figure ran across Andrews' field of vision in front of the car. For a moment he thought it was the skier. Then the figure was leaning over him, hands braced on the twisted door, and he saw that it was Nels Graham.

35

Andrews turned to examine Pat, as Graham and one of the agents who had arrived with him worked to force open the door on the driver's side of the wrecked sports car. Graham's long arm snaked in and he switched off the ignition to avoid a fire.

"I'm all right, I think," Pat said dazedly. "At least I don't hurt anywhere."

"The woman has a head injury," one of the agents said.

Pat raised a hand to her forehead and was surprised to feel the slight swelling and see blood on her fingers.

"It doesn't look serious," Andrews assured her.

The door came unstuck and creaked stiffly open. The grating sound jarred Andrews' mind back to full capacity for reason. "Underwood's up there dead," he said. He watched Graham's face, flushed from cold and effort, give a slight muscular spasm in reaction to the news. Yet he didn't seem at all surprised.

"Either of you hurt too badly to get out?" he asked Andrews.

"I don't think so." Andrews' right knee was sore from where it had jammed into the dashboard, but other than that he could perceive no pain or numbness.

With Graham's help, he climbed shakily out of the car. Then both men helped Pat slide across the bucket seats and get out on Andrews' side. The door on her side of the car was wedged tight against one of the trees. She was trembling as she managed to stand and lean against Andrews.

"Sit down for a while," he told her, and held her hand as he led her to the car Graham had arrived in. He opened one of the rear doors and she crawled inside to slump on the spacious back seat. The car's interior was still warm, and Andrews knew that she'd be asleep soon. She smiled up at him, a luxurious smile. She felt safe now.

"Over here," Graham called.

Andrews left Pat and joined Graham and another agent at the side of the road. At their feet was the fallen skier. He had been a broad, muscular man. One leg and his neck were bent at grotesque angles, and one side of his knitted ski mask was saturated with blood. Graham knelt and removed the ski mask and goggles to reveal the face of the dead man.

The man was not Martin Karpp. Though his face was marked with blood, his features still were discernible. He was not anyone Andrews recognized.

Graham let out a trailing breath that condensed to steam in the cool air. He seemed to know the man but said nothing.

"There's at least one more up on the mountain," Andrews told him. "Who are they?"

"There are two men up there," Graham said, ignoring Andrews' question for the moment. He looked at his three agents and nodded. One of them walked to the car where Pat was, opened the trunk and returned with three high-powered rifles, along with, Andrews was surprised to see, a submachine gun and spare ammunition clips.

"I noticed a motel just this side of Perith," Graham said to Andrews, "the Snow King."

Graham seemed to consider for a few seconds, then he addressed a tall agent with tiny brown eyes and high, Indian cheekbones. "Manwell," he said, "drive the senator and Miss

Colombo to the Snow King Motel. See that they're comfortably situated, then return here."

Manwell nodded impassively and stood waiting.

"I'd like to know what the hell is going on," Andrews said. He suddenly felt incredibly exhausted. Whatever vitality had been provided by the adrenaline his heart had pumped in the past fifteen minutes was leaving him.

"Please wait for me at the motel, Senator," Graham said in an official yet oddly pleading voice. "I'll explain everything to you there later and you'll understand. And I'd rather that you and Miss Colombo talk to no one until I get there. You'll understand that request, too, after I've explained."

Andrews looked at the motionless armed agents and thought about the men still up on the mountain. This wasn't the place to waste Graham's time with senatorial demands for names and reasons. He nodded his agreement. Carrying one of the rifles loosely beneath his right arm, Manwell led Andrews back to the agency car.

At the motel, Manwell took care of the registration. He returned from the office and drove the car to near the end of the building's west leg and parked. Out of courtesy or caution, he opened the door to the room and looked around before ushering them inside.

"You won't be disturbed here, Senator," he said. With an unreadable glance at Pat, who was seated on the edge of the bed, he left. Andrews locked the door behind Manwell, heard the agent's car fling gravel.

Andrews stood looking down at Pat, and the questions boiling in his mind seemed less important. "We're alive," he said, his flat voice edged with incredulity.

"I don't feel alive," she answered. After unzipping her boots, she eased them off gingerly with her toes, unwilling to bend deeply enough from the high bed to use her hands. The boots fell noisily to the floor with two blunt, final thuds that seemed to signal the end of the ordeal. Finis. And thank God.

On the drive with Manwell down the mountain, Andrews had looked forward to lowering himself into a tub of hot water. Now he discovered that he was too exhausted even for that. He stretched out on the bed next to Pat. They slept.

And it was morning.

A telephone was ringing in the distance, over and over, with sadistic persistence. As Andrews sought and found wakefulness, the ringing became louder. It was coming from the phone beside the bed. His right arm stretched out and his hand closed on the receiver and dragged it to his ear.

"Senator Andrews?" a voice asked.

Andrews croaked his identity, cleared his throat and repeated himself.

"This is Nels Graham, Senator. Can we talk alone? In the coffee shop?"

Andrews focused his blurred vision on Pat Colombo. She was still asleep, breathing deeply and regularly, her face turned away from the sunlight beaming in through the space between two twisted venetian-blind slats. Exactly one half of her pillow was starkly illuminated, like the bright side of a planet.

"Give me about ten minutes," Andrews said.

"Take your time, Senator."

Andrews hung up the phone and quietly got out of bed. The cold from the concrete floor beneath the carpet seeped to his stockinged feet and brought him completely awake. As he moved toward the bathroom, he found that his right knee was sore enough to cause him to limp. All of his muscles ached, as if he'd endured a beating. Clumsily, he began to unbutton the wrinkled shirt in which he'd slept. He was ready now for that steaming bath.

Twenty minutes later, Andrews was seated across from Graham in a corner booth in the Snow King's coffee shop. It was past ten o'clock, and they were the only customers. Pat was still asleep. Andrews had left her a note in case she awoke while he was gone. She wasn't to worry about him, and she was to wait in the room for his return.

Andrews realized for the first time how hungry he was, and while Graham had only coffee, he ordered the pancake special. He began gorging himself while Graham explained.

"It hinges on this," Graham said. "Paul Liggett existed. I mean actually existed. He was not one of Martin Karpp's original personalities."

Andrews downed a large swallow of coffee, as yet unable to fathom the implications of that statement. "Was Liggett the man on the mountain, the dead skier?"

"Yes and no," Graham answered. "The man you killed with the car was Brian Haller. He was a CIA agent."

Andrews stopped a bite of pancake halfway to his mouth, suddenly stupefied. If Paul Liggett actually existed . . . Then his mind turned up a recollection. "It seems to me that I *have* seen the dead man, Haller, somewhere before."

Graham nodded. "Probably you saw him in New York, when he was trying to scare you off his trail, before trying to kill you when he saw that you weren't scaring. Four years ago Haller was part of an ultrasecret splinter group of the CIA, a group that took it upon themselves to attempt to alter the course of history. They decided that Governor Drake was a candidate who would sway enough voters to influence the election against the incumbent President. They didn't want that. They decided to assassinate Drake."

No longer hungry, Andrews sat holding his coffee cup in both hands and staring at Graham, grasping ramifications. "Did the President—"

"Did he know?" Graham finished for him. "Did he approve, even tacitly?" He shrugged. "We don't know. Probably we could never prove it if we did know. He's out of office now, a respected elder statesman. It will stay that way."

"This splinter group," Andrews said, "what was their method?"

"They culled the hundreds of threatening letters and hate mail that Drake—like the other presidential candidates—received and routinely passed on to the authorities. Out of these letters, they settled on several from Martin Karpp. They decided that his letters definitely were to be taken seriously, and he lived near New Jersey, which was on Drake's campaign itinerary. Instead of taking the routine precautions against Karpp, they kept his existence a secret from the rest of the authorities, and they contrived to use him as their tool. He was closely observed, surreptitiously studied, painstakingly analyzed by psychiatrists. He turned out to be everything they wanted and more.

"Finally Brian Haller, who somewhat resembled Karpp, was assigned to 'affix' himself as Paul Liggett onto Karpp's ménage of personalities. Haller was extensively trained by experts in psychology, given specific instructions, even given a duplicate key to Karpp's apartment. As Liggett, he made late-night phone calls to Karpp, entered the apartment when Karpp was away and in Karpp's childish printing made entries in Karpp's diary and notebooks, added to and altered the graffiti on the walls. Eventually Karpp came to accept Liggett as another of his puzzle-piece, interconnected identities. And Liggett was tailor-made by experts to convince Karpp's Jay Jefferson personality to make good his threat to assassinate Governor Drake."

Andrews imagined how it must have been for Martin Karpp, already unbalanced, confused and agonized; deliberately kept that way, his psychosis intensified and brought to bear for a lethal purpose not his own. If ever a man actually had been possessed by demons, that man was Karpp. And the demons were real.

"It worked, as you know," Graham said, his voice still modulated for privacy. "Drake was shot and killed, and Karpp was captured, as they'd planned he would be. As details of his private life became known, it was obvious that he was mentally ill. Everything he said was suspect or flatly disbelieved. There was little if any doubt of his guilt. It remained only for him to be declared legally insane and committed. Which is what happened. All as planned."

"Then?" Andrews asked.

Graham smiled tightly. "Then nothing. Until your friend Dr. Larsen decided to research multiple personality and came to you so he could interview Karpp. That wasn't too bad. But in the course of his research, he began to dig into each of Karpp's past lives, the histories of each of Karpp's separate personalities as they'd existed in New York before the Drake assassination. That was something the real planners of Drake's murder couldn't tolerate, so they eliminated Dr. Larsen."

"And in their eyes, I took his place," Andrews said.

"Exactly. Haller and friends couldn't be sure that either of you wouldn't get onto the fact that the Liggett personality was fabricated *outside* of Karpp's mind."

Then Andrews fully understood. There had been no Paul Liggett until shortly before the assassination. And no one in Manhattan had mentioned him, either directly or indirectly. He hadn't existed physically as had the others, because Martin Karpp had never acted him out.

"It was only a matter of time," Graham said, "until first Larsen, then you, would realize that of all Karpp's personalities, Paul Liggett was the only one who hadn't any verifiable past."

'But if you knew all this *time*—"

"We could suspect and nothing more, Senator. And we've long been suspicious of events surrounding the Drake assassination, the only one of several that hasn't prompted public furor and disbelief. It was too well planned and carried out for that, you see." Graham finished his coffee, waited quietly while the waitress refilled both his cup and Andrews'.

"In Manhattan," he continued, "we'd hoped that Haller would fall for the bait of your substitute at the Hayes Hotel. And he did put on a phony murder attempt that suggested he might think he'd actually killed you. But they were getting desperate by then, and we eventually saw through it. They only wanted us to think they'd taken the bait, so they could safely go after you here, at your cabin. Once we realized what was happening, a squad of men was dispatched to observe and protect you. Underwood arrived ahead of us and was supposed to set up the operation."

Andrews remembered that he'd found Underwood's body well above the cabin. "But no one told me what was going on," he said. "And you weren't going to tell me. You were using me—and Pat Colombo—as bait this time."

"I don't know that I'd express it in such accusatory terms," Graham said uncomfortably.

"I would," Andrews said.

Graham ignored his persistence. "Haller and his henchman found out Underwood was watching over you and killed him. You know most of the rest."

"Most?"

Graham nodded. "My agents caught up with Haller's two associates on the mountain yesterday. They resisted and had to be killed."

"Had to be?"

Graham's face remained devoid of decipherable expression. "Of course."

Andrews rested his hands palms down on the table. He saw that the scratches and cuts on them were now vivid. "So that ends it," he said.

"Not quite, Senator. Which is really why I needed to talk with you."

Andrews could see the almost imperceptible signs on Graham's features, sense the accelerated but harnessed tempo of his thinking. There was a humming power and competency in the man. With a politician's instincts, Andrews got the distinct impression that Graham was about to propose a deal. The sight of the half-eaten pancakes in front of him suddenly nauseated Andrews. He averted his eyes and pushed the plate away.

"The two men on the mountain chose to be killed rather than surrender," Graham told Andrews. "And you've killed Haller. Proof against the former President or any peripheral participants in the plot would be difficult if not impossible to obtain. The media would dig and sensationalize. There would be a colossal mess that would unjustifiably soil the reputation of the entire agency and impair our efficiency. Nothing positive would result from it."

"You keep saying 'would,' " Andrews said. "As if there were some sort of choice." But he knew there was a choice. Always a choice. That was what Graham was offering. The operation here at Perith could be cleaned up, kept secret. The dead could be reported killed in other ways, in other places. Andrews waited for Graham to play his best, his most convincing cards.

"Naturally," Graham went on, "once the media start they don't stop until there's nothing left but bones. And they don't care whose bones. If any part of the story comes out, all of it inevitably will. And you have much to lose, Senator, from the revelation of your relationship with Miss Colombo."

"Only a career," Andrews said ironically.

"I notice you didn't mention your marriage."

"No," Andrews said, "I didn't."

Graham studied him from across the table, as if considering telling him something more, then deciding against it. "You have an extremely bright future in this country's politics, Senator," Graham said. "We both know that. It would be tragic for something like this to thwart your desires. And I understand your desires better than you might think. A tempest would be provoked that would incriminate only the dead. What difference would it make? Of the living, only you can be harmed."

"And the agency."

"Us too, yes. I mentioned that. It's in our best interest to keep a lid on the thing. Believe me, Senator, it's a Pandora's box; there'd be no going back."

Andrews knew that from a practical point of view Graham was right. From a practical point of view. He also knew that he had a few cards of his own to play, but as yet he didn't know how to play them.

"I'm going to take a short walk," Andrews said. "To think. Will you be here when I return?"

"Right here," Graham said. "Drinking another cup of coffee."

As Andrews stood up, Graham added, "We don't have very long to decide, Senator."

Andrews returned to the coffee shop within fifteen minutes. He had walked the snow-cleared main street of Perith, then a short distance toward the mountain, among the quiet pines and snow that was unbroken but for his own black footprints. He'd made his decision.

"I keep thinking about justice," he said, as he again slid into the booth across from Graham.

"Justice?"

"That's what's missing," Andrews said, "but it doesn't have to be. Not entirely."

Graham smiled, the smile of a man who thought more about expediency than justice. "A condition?"

"Yes," Andrews said. "I'll be silent if a condition is agreed upon. Only one condition. And we both know that once I've kept my silence for even a short period of time, I'll have to continue that silence."

"I presume then, Senator, that once the condition is met, it also will be irreversible."

"There'll be no need to reverse it," Andrews said. "I want Martin Karpp released. Officially pardoned."

Graham appeared stunned. "They'll say that he might kill again."

"He would never have killed the first time if he hadn't been driven to it by experts."

"Imagine the public outcry."

"Public outcries and puzzlement have arisen over previous, less deserved pardons," Andrews said. "Things pass."

Graham pursed his lips and bowed his head. "Justice . . ." he muttered thoughtfully. As if in amazement, he stared up at Andrews and said, "Justice really *is* what you want."

"I almost died yesterday," Andrews told him. "I'm less concerned now with political considerations."

"Then you actually would let your tenuous personal life be revealed in order to set the record straight and effect Karpp's release?"

"If you don't agree to do it the easy way."

"Can we be assured of Miss Colombo's silence? She'd be protecting you, of course, as well as herself and your relationship."

"I can guarantee her silence," Andrews said, "by seeing to it that for her own sake she never knows all of this."

Graham drummed his manicured fingers once, loudly, on the table. "We have a bargain," he said.

Andrews was surprised. "Just like that? Without relaying the request? Do you have the authority?"

Graham showed his thin smile. "I have the authority." He stood up and shook hands with Andrews. "If you'll excuse me, Senator, I have to supervise the delicate matter of dissemblance."

"Is that agency jargon for covering your tracks?" Andrews

asked, unable to resist putting an edge of contempt in his voice.

"Yes," Graham admitted. "In politics it's called redefining your position."

He left Andrews then, moving with controlled briskness and purpose toward the door, in as much of a hurry as he probably ever got.

Andrews' coffee cup from breakfast was still on the table. The waitress walked over and dutifully refilled it, commenting that it was nice that the snow had stopped. Andrews agreed. He sat and drank his coffee. When he was finished, he would go back to the room and awaken Pat. Then they would get in the Jeep that had been brought down from the mountain, and they would begin the long trip home.

36

Nels Graham stood and watched the Jeep carrying Andrews and Pat Colombo disappear around a soiled snowbank beyond the end of Perith's main street. A low haze of exhaust fumes lay over the cindered pavement, then dissipated. Graham wanted to be positive that the senator had left, so that he could be sure of his silence. He needed to be sure.

Lighting a cigarette and dropping the match to hiss to extinction in an ice-flecked puddle, Graham turned to walk back to his car. He was satisfied. Knots had been tied in every loose end. Haller was dead. And Graham had seen to it that the two men up on the mountain also died. He had shot one of them himself, though the man was about to surrender. With the other agents along, Graham hadn't had a choice. Just as he'd had no choice but to order the deaths in New York. As well as the deaths of Andrews' wife and her lover. And Underwood's death.

But it was over. The rest of the splinter group now were safe. Andrews would keep his silence, as would the dead. And Karpp would be released, of course. The media would be in a frenzy over Karpp. But what difference would that make? Graham flipped his cigarette away before getting into the car. What difference did any of it make now?

Breathing freely for the first time since he'd heard of Dr. Dana Larsen, he put the idling car in drive and headed up the mountain.

EPILOGUE
March 17, 1992

Martin Karpp moved inward from the edge of the crowd. He was wearing a policeman's uniform and a policeman's holstered revolver; Alan Hobson had obtained them for him. Martin Karpp didn't know how or from where, and he chose not to think about the crusty brownish-red stain on the cuff of the right sleeve. He smiled at an attractive young woman holding her infant on her shoulders. Then he saw the dark-blue uniform cap of another policeman in his path, and he slightly altered his direction. Security was tight here. Martin Karpp was part of it. Or seemed to be.

On a raised wooden platform draped in red, white and blue stood former CIA director, former ambassador to France and adviser to the President, and now candidate for the Republican nomination for President of the United States, Nelson Horatio Graham. Tall and gray, pugnacious and indignant about the plight of Middle America, Graham was grinding out his number one campaign speech with well-rehearsed passion. He was the favorite in tomorrow's Illinois primary.

As soon as he'd come to national prominence and his image began to appear with regularity in newspapers and on TV, Karpp had remembered Graham. He had seen him once in Manhattan on Forty-seventh Street, the day before Jay Jefferson shot Governor Drake, talking to Paul Liggett. At the time, it hadn't struck Karpp as impossible to see Liggett talking to a stranger, even though they were involved in what obviously was an argument. But Karpp remembered that moment because it was the only time he actually had seen Paul Liggett, or any of the others. When recently he'd discovered the identity of the man who'd been talking with Liggett, he had thought for a long time about things. Then he had reached a decision.

Karpp was within fifty feet of the raised platform now, on the inner edge of the crowd. A man in a dark business suit, standing behind and to the left of Graham, glanced at him, then saw the uniform and let his eyes slide away. Graham was on the subject of inflation now, building his speech to its climax. Oh, he was a skilled deceiver. Martin Karpp had heard the speech several times and knew.

When Nelson Graham thanked the crowd and raised both long arms high in the air in anticipation of victory, a bedlam of wild applause and cheering exploded from the crowd, prompted by professionals strategically planted by Graham's campaign committee.

It was the moment.

Martin Karpp and no one else drew his revolver and flung his uniform cap aside. He had planned to scream whatever it was that John Wilkes Booth had shouted when he'd killed Lincoln, but at that instant he forgot the words he had so carefully rehearsed. There was too much noise to be heard anyway.

The vulnerable crowd around Martin Karpp caused a second's hesitation in the Secret Service agents assigned to protect Nelson Graham. Karpp got one shot away, saw Graham's astounded expression, saw him slump forward onto the lectern that collapsed beneath him.

Then came the blackness and pain. Martin Karpp had never felt such pain. Some detached part of him remembered disturbing a nest of wasps while scything weeds as a boy, the terrible stinging that wouldn't stop. Only this was so much worse. This was like the countless mouths of the angry and starving, devouring him. Death had never been so welcome.

When presidential candidate Jerry Andrews, at Chicago's Westbury Hotel, heard the news of Nelson Graham's death, he immediately canceled his remaining Illinois campaign appearances. He was sickened. Saddened. During the course of the primaries he had come to respect Nelson Graham's positions on the issues as well as his ability as a campaigner. Andrews made the appropriate comments to the media, and he meant them.

And he knew that, but for his efforts, Martin Karpp still would be locked harmlessly away in the Belmont sanitarium.

As far as Andrews knew, Karpp had never seen Nelson Graham in person. There was no way he could have discovered Graham's role in his release so many years ago.

Andrews felt far away from that time, from events that he now seldom thought about other than fleetingly. And it had been a long time ago, and had involved a younger, different Jerry Andrews. Now he walked stiffly from the effects of the helicopter accident, and his hair was almost completely gray. He was developing a slight stomach paunch despite a stringent diet.

Different people in a different time, and yet Karpp had been driven by some vestige of that time to murder Nelson Graham. Andrews refused to believe that Karpp had chosen Graham as his victim by some bizarre coincidence.

Then why? What could he have known?

Though Andrews couldn't quite capture it in his consciousness, he knew that with Karpp's murder of Graham, some remote connection had been made in his mind.

Andrews' campaign manager Jack Copperud knocked twice and then entered the suite. "We've wrapped up activities for the day, Senator," he said, dropping the Chicago evening papers onto the sofa.

"Good. I don't feel like talking about the latest polls."

"They don't mean anything now anyway," Copperud said. "Tomorrow it's a new campaign." He lifted a weary arm and lowered it heavily. "Good night, Senator."

Andrews told him good night and watched him leave. The suite was quiet. Copperud had looked exhausted, Andrews thought, and decided that he'd look that way himself tomorrow if he didn't get to bed.

Beside his sleeping wife Pat, Andrews lay awake for hours. Until finally he was visited by understanding.

He remembered the lack of surprise on Graham's face when he'd been told that Underwood was dead. And he remembered that same younger Graham standing over a dead skier on an icy mountainside, informing his agents with casual certainty that there were two more armed men up on the mountain. Two exactly. Though Andrews had been dazed at the time and the words hadn't registered, he could recall them now as if Graham had spoken them here in this room only minutes ago. And now he realized their implication, what Graham at the time must have known. Subsequently the two men had been killed, not apprehended.

And somehow Martin Karpp had discovered what Andrews only now was surmising.

Andrews got out of bed and mixed himself a drink. Then he stood at the window, looking out at the myriad lights of Chicago that were like a bright extension of the galaxy above.

He was, and would remain, the only one who understood the true nature of Martin Karpp's crime, the completion of the circle.